A *Prayer* IN THE *Garden*

EFREM TRIPLETT

Scriptor House LLC

2810 N Church St Wilmington, Delaware, 19802

www.scriptorhouse.com

Phone: +1302-205-2043

Published by Scriptor House LLC

Paperback ISBN: **979-8-88692-030-7**

eBook ISBN: **979-8-88692-031-4**

CHAPTER 1
Childhood

As a child, I always wondered how my life would turn out. My dad once told me that I would be a beautiful housewife with kids. My mother said that I would be a clothes designer because I loved to wear dresses. We lived in a beautiful house in Florida. It had three bedrooms with four floors, including the attic and the basement. My room was up the spiral stairs, around the balustrade, and down the hallway. My parent's room was just down the hallway as soon as you reach the top of the stairs. The room to the left was a room used for my dad's office. He owned a security company, and my mom was a college professor.

My childhood friend Mia lived just across the street from us. I played with her every opportunity I got. We loved dressing up our barbie dolls together on our front porches and chasing each other around some trees. She would come to my house almost every day after school.

My parents were once going to a local church, but the church ended up disintegrating after the pastor was shot to death while leaving the church. That hit my dad hard because the pastor had been his pastor for over fifteen years. Pastor Brown once helped my parents through a financial struggle. He vowed not to join another church and not get close to get close to anymore pastors.

I missed the way my father used to chase me up and down the stairs, acting like he was a monster. My dad was always so playful, but when he was serious, he was serious. I remember when he got mad at me when I took his car keys and purposely threw them out the window. I was five years old at the time.

"What did you do that for Ailina!" He screamed. That was one of the loudest screams I ever heard from him. I gotta admit, I was scared like a mouse in a snake pit.

"I'm sorry daddy," I said with a whimper. He couldn't stay mad at me for long. I was his little princess. He picked me up and sat me down on my bed. He ran his fingers through my long silky light-brown hair. Then he looked down at me and said,

"You have the most beautiful eyes Li Li." He smiled, looking into my diamond-shaped hazel brown eyes with long curly eyelashes.

My mother was of mixed race. Black, Asian and Caucasian. My dad was black and Native American. He had brown -colored skin and stood six feet two. My mother had very light skin, and she wasn't that tall. Only about five feet five.

"Now are you ready for bed?" he asked.

"Yes daddy," I answered. He then pulled the covers halfway off my bed and I laid down. He snuggled me under the covers. My mother walked in moments later in her black and white stiped nightgown.

"Is she ready Marlo?" my mother asked.

"Oh, hey honey. Yes, she is." She walked toward my bed and sat next to me. My dad walked across my room and closed my Purple and white polka dotted curtains.

"Hi mama!" I said excitedly.

"How's my baby girl?"

"Fine, I'm just getting ready for bed." My dad walked back over to my bed and sat next to my mother. I loved it when it was just the three of us in my room. I felt secure, safe and untouchable. Whenever I was with both of my parents, it felt like I was with Jesus and the virgin Mary. They always stayed in my room with me until I fell asleep. Part of that was because my dad was very protective of me. Sometimes they would sing Gospel songs to me or read short stories from one of my children's books collections of my bookshelf until I was fast asleep.

"Are you ready for kindergarten, sweetheart?" My dad asked. I put the biggest smile on my face. And nodded up and down.

"Good, ah, oooooh, I feel a tickle coming on." He held his hands up, as if he was gonna attack me. Then he tickled me. I laughed so hard I thought I was gonna pee on myself.

"Jan, you wanna sing her a song?" My mom began to sing. She had the most beautiful voice. It was very soft and very sweet. As she sang, there was a huge smile on my face. Moments later, I began to feel myself falling fast asleep. My eyes were getting very heavy and low then lower... then lower... until I fell asleep.

***

I started kindergarten the next morning, my teacher, Mr. Taylor always told me I was his favorite. That was because I was a well-behaved student. He used to hold my hand as we walked down the hallway when it was time to go to recess. He was average in height, had short wavy dark-black hair, was in his mid to late twenties and had a medium build. He was well shaved, but he never shaved off his small mustache.

My childhood friend Mia went to the same school as I did. We had different teachers, but we always played together outside. She was always Trying to make me feel better at recess when I was upset about something.

So, my first day was exciting. That morning My mom cooked me a small breakfast. Two sausage links, a biscuit, and some eggs. She then dressed me in my pink and white dress with the white fashion belt around it. My hair was combed straight down with a pink ribbon tied in it. I couldn't wait to meet the other kids and play with the in the classroom.

Mr. Taylor waited for us by the classroom door. I saw the other kids running around, playing, and laughing. My mom and dad walked up to him.

"Well, hello there little one. You must be Ailina?" He greeted us with the biggest smile. I just smiled back.

"Yes, I'm Mr. Chauhan, and this is my wife Mrs. Chauhan. We're her parents." My dad reached out to shake Mr. Taylor's hand. Mr. Taylor then returned the handshake.

"It's a pleasure to meet you both," he said, shaking both of their hands.

We walked into the classroom, and Mr. Taylor gave us a tour. On one side of the room, there were small round tables with different colored chairs surrounding them. On the other side, there were kind of like a play area with toys. Toy trucks, stuffed animals, dolls etc. there was also a bookshelf with a number of different children's books. The walls were painted yellow, and the ceiling just plain white with a chandelier hanging from the middle. Instead of hardwood floors, there was blue carpet throughout the entire room. At the far back of the classroom, there was a rabbit inside a cage sitting on the counter.

"This is our classroom pet," Mr. Taylor said. "I don't know what to name him yet. He's still a baby."

"We can name him Veggie," I said. "I know rabbits are vegetarian." He leaned down towards me replied,

"Well, that makes sense, Ailina. We'll just name him Veggie then. How did you know rabbits are vegetarian?"

"I have a book that my mommy and daddy read to me about a rabbit who loves to eat carrots, lettuce, and leaves. And the rabbit's name is Veggie."

"That's one of her favorite books," my mom said.

"She seems like a very bright child. I know your kid is gonna love it in this class."

My parents hugged and kissed me and told me to be a good girl, and then they left the room.

"Okay, kids, come over her on the carpet and pop a squat so we can meet one another, said Mr. Taylor." We sat in the circle and introduced ourselves. I had so much fun that day. I met a little girl named Toa. She was always so nice to me. Every time lunch came around, she always gave me some of her food. I believed it was her way of saying to me, "I want to be friends forever."

My kindergarten year was very smooth and fun. By the second grade, Toa and Mia were still my friends. I was very happy. We played together every chance we got, always running up and down the slides, pushing one another on the swing set, and laughing at boys getting into fights.

Childhood was awesome. However, all that was about to change when I got home from school one day. It was in the middle of May, and the school year was ending soon. I was eight almost nine years old.

***

I asked my mom and dad if I could play with Mia outside.

"Don't go too far honey. I have to do your hair for school tomorrow," my mother said.

"Okay mom." I put on my shoes and ran out the door. Mia was already on her porch, combing her hair.

I waved at her to come over to where I was. She was smiling while walking towards me. She was walking as if she was coming to receiving a lifetime achievement award. I saw an all-black old school Camaro zooming down the street. It was also swerving down the street. It just so happened that Mia was crossing the street at the same time. The car hit her and kept going. I didn't see who was inside. It happened so fast. I screamed in horror, Like I saw Jason or Freddy Krueger or somebody.

My mom and dad ran out the house when they heard the screams.

"Lina, Lina what happened!" my dad yelled. I just turned around and ran to him. "Jan, take her in the house! Take her in the house Jan!" he ordered. I just start yelling,

"NOOOO, DADDY, I DON'T WANNA GO IN THE HOUSE. I WANT TO PLAY WITH MIA!"

"Mia is hurt Li Li, just go in the house. Just go!" My mom picked me up and took me in the house. "Come on honey." I heard my dad yelling out, "Someone call an ambulance!"

I was in my room looking out the window. I saw an ambulance, a fire truck, two squad cars, and an FBI vehicle. I couldn't see Mia because the fire truck was blocking my view. I saw her mother holding Mia's dad, crying. She then dropped to the ground, and Mia's dad picked her up and held her. Then she was crying.

My dad came in moments later. He had a look on his face as if he was having a heart attack. I got off my bed and walked towards him.

"Is Mia okay daddy?" He was silent. That was when I knew she was gone. I ran in his arms and yelled, "NOOOO, DADDY SHE CAN'T BE DEAD!" I was so stunned because I never thought something like that could actually happen to a young girl.

There were lots of people at Mia's funeral. Toa, other friends from school, and even Mr. Taylor were there. She looked so beautiful in her yellow and black dress. She had white stockings and yellow ballet shoes on. Her hair was done in curls, and her dark skin still looked so smooth and beautiful.

Months after the funeral, Mia's parents came over to our house with two large boxes. In those boxes were some of Mia's belongings- Hair combs, brushes, bow ties, shoes, a picture of Mia, and some clothes. Her parents also came over to break the news that they were moving out of the state.

They couldn't stand not being able to look out their window and watch Mia play outside. They wanted to leave so they could get a new start and try to forget the past. So, they figured giving me her things and leaving town would be the best solution.

Mia and her parents had lived in their house since she was born. Her parents moved there when they got married. My parents moved on the block around the same time. I was nearly one. So, they had been friends for that long.

"I wish you both the best. And I pray that God heal your broken hearts," My mom said. As she was crying. My parents also gave them a large sum of money to make sure they would be okay on the road. My parents were really close to them. On hot summer days, my dad would throw a barbecue party and would invite them over. Mia and I would play in the backyard, climbing trees and playing hide-and-seek. So, it was heartbreaking to my parents when they decided to move. I remembered one time during a barbecue party when Mia fell and scrapped her leg while running. They all exchanged hugs and cried. They went about their way, and we never saw them again.

CHAPTER 2
A Turn of Events

Two years later, I finally got over Mia's death. Toa and I were still going to the same school and still friends. She touched my heart when she told me she will be my new best friend. We were now in the fourth grade. We both were starting to develop as young women. The fourth grade was a pretty interesting year. Boys began to like me because of my beauty. My hair was halfway down my back, and my eyes got even more hazel brown. I started to develop breasts, and my thighs were just a little thicker. I grew a little taller too, standing about four feet four.

I entered my second year of middle school, and I just developed even more. Toa and I only had one class together. I developed an interest in boys, but I wasn't that type of girl. Students used to call me Li Li the good girl because I didn't do what they did or rarely got into trouble. My mom and dad were watching me very closely, making sure I didn't get myself in any trouble.

"Look Ailina, you're a young lady now, and these boys got their eyes on you," my dad said.

"And how you know that dad?"

"I was a young boy before, Li Li, and how you think I got with your mother?" My mom laughed, but for some reason I didn't find it funny. My dad was right about that. Boys did have their eyes on me. When I walked down the hallways, I saw other boys looking at my backside when I walked past them.

I woke up one night to a phone call. It had to be about one in the morning. I got up and turned on my lamp. When I answered the phone, it was Toa.

"Girl, why are you calling me so late? You know I can't have phone calls after nine O'clock."

"I know, girl. I just gotta tell you what happened!" She sounded like she was about to tell me she won a million bucks.

"Wutsup Chica?" I said tiredly.

"Andrew and Sandra broke up." I sat up on my bed. This was some news because Andrew and Sandra had been the admired couple for a while.

"What happened between them?" I asked.

"I just got off the phone with Sandra and she told me that she caught him kissing the Erica chick in the hallway."

"Are you freaking kidding me! He was kissing that hoe?"

"Yep, according to Sandra. She was crying so hard on the phone with me, gurlll. I felt so bad for her."

"Did she really say it was over?"

"Yes, she did." I heard my parents' bedroom door open. Then I whispered to Toa,

"I gotta go. We'll talk at school." Then I hung up the phone, turned my lamp off, and lay back down. I could tell by those soft footsteps that it was my mother. She went to the bathroom and went back to bed.

***

There was tension between Sandra and Andrew the next morning at school. At lunch, it was all bad. Toa, Sandra and I were at the table talking. Sandra was still upset at the fact that Andrew had cheated on her.

"I just can't believe that dirty bastard!" she yelled. Andrew walked over to the table and tapped Sandra on the table.

"Hey, can I talk to you for a second?" He asked.

"I don't think so, Andrew Just go away," Sandra responded. He held his head down and sat next to her. "Listen, I know you're mad at me. I just wanna say I'm sorry. That kiss didn't mean anything between us. I didn't come over here for your pity or your forgiveness, but can we at least still talk?" Sandra just looked the other way smacked her lips. Toa and I both looked at her like, 'well, what are going to do?' She just kept quiet. Erica then came over with her little clique.

"Hey Andrew." She wrapped her arms around him. I could tell by the look on his face that he was disgusted. Sandra started at him like 'I know you're not going to let her do that.'

"Erica don't do that, get your hands off me," Andrew said.

"What's wrong baby? You need me to cheer you up?" She wrapped her arms around him again and stared at Sandra. Andrew jumped up and yelled,

"Erica I'm serious. Keep your hands off me!"

"Oh, I get it. You're still sprung on this tramp," she said, pointing at Sandra. That pissed her off. Sandra jumped up and said,

"Bitch, who you think you're talking to! I will slap the sh…

"Sandra, no girl! Don't get yourself in trouble. She's not worth it, I said. Sandra took a deep breath and sat back down slowly. Andrew looked at Erica and said,

"Listen, Erica, do us a favor and get away from here before things get bad."

"Really Andrew? She replied.

"Yes, really!"

"You weren't saying that when you kissed me!"

"Whatever Erica. You can't kiss anyway. Get the hell away from here." She and her clique turned around and just left. I saw the anger in Sandra's eyes. She looked as if she was ready to kill someone.

Andrew sat back down and looked at Sandra and said, "Like I was saying, you don't have to forgive me or take me back. However, can you still just say hi to me in the hallway or something?" She looked at us like, 'what should I do?' Andrew got up and said, "Bye Sandra," and walked off. Sandra jumped and went after him. She ended up forgiving him, and they were back together.

***

At home that day, I was talking to Sandra on the phone. I was sitting on my bed, listening to my radio. I put on my Zen records. The sun was still shining through my window.

"Did you see how my baby stood up for me?" Sandra said. "Oh my goodness he told that hoe something about herself."

"He surely did, gurl. What made you wanna take him back?" I asked.

"Well, he wasn't begging like a dog. He acknowledged the fact that he was wrong, and that's a turn on for me for some reason. And besides, I still love him." As she was talking, I was smiling and polishing my nails.

"I can't believe you called her a bitch. I thought you was gonna slap the taste out her mouth gurl."

"I was until you stopped me."

"I just didn't want you to get into trouble."

"Why you got your music so loud? Can you turn it down?"

"Oh yeah, my bad. I love me some Phenomenal Zen." I got up and turned down my radio.

"You know Billy likes you, right?" she said.

"Are you serious, Billy Rodgers?"

"Yep, he told me after school yesterday." I got excited because I had a crush on him since the beginning of the school year. "Let me give you a little heads up my friend. He's gonna ask you to the valentine's dance tomorrow. Act like you're surprised because I told him that I wasn't gonna tell you."

"Oh, my lord, you can't be serious," I said, as if someone brought me a canary diamond ring. Suddenly, there was a knock on my door. "Come in." I yelled. It was my mother.

"Come down for dinner, sweetheart," she said with a soft voice.

"Okay momma, here I come." She closed my door back and left. "I gotta go gurl. So, I'll see you tomorrow at school?"

"Yeah, see you tomorrow, Chica." We hung up, and I went downstairs.

The smell of pot roast and potatoes with steamed vegetables hit my nose as soon as I opened the door. I joined my parents for dinner at the table. My dad always said grace before we ate. Dinner time was our time together. A time to speak what was on our minds and laugh about silly things.

"Who were you talking to on the phone, Ailina?" my mom asked.

"I was talking to Sandra. She was telling me that her and her boyfriend got back together."

"You young people are driving me up a wall with this boyfriend and girlfriend stuff," my dad said. "God never said to have a boyfriend and girlfriend. He said to let every man have one *wife* and every woman to have one *husband*."

"Dad, you and momma was boyfriends and girlfriends at first."

"That's because we weren't saved yet," he replied. "We didn't know God the way we know him know." We just continued talking about God and what the Word of God says about relationships and marriages.

My mom fixed her eyes on me from across the table and said,

"Ailina, listen. I wanna tell you this because one day you will be married. The best gift you can give your new husband is a body that has never been touched. Don't degrade yourself by letting boys have their way with you. Your body is the temple of the holy spirit. If a man can't respect your wishes and wait for marriage to have sex, he's not the one for you. If he doesn't have Christ as the head of his life, most definitely, he's not the one. Do you understand Li Li?"

"Yes ma'am." She smiled at me and began eating her food. Her words to me were just so powerful. It was powerful because they came from the word of God. I didn't understand how powerful they were until later on in my adult life.

"Your mother and I have something else to tell you Li," my dad said. "We've decided to go back to church and sit under the leadership of another pastor. We talked about it last night."

"Okay, do you have one in mind that we can go to?"

"We were thinking about that church over on the east side of town. We heard that the pastor of that church is very wonderful and teaches only the Word of God with clarity and understanding."

"Okay, that sounds good. What made you decide that, dad?"

"Faith comes by hearing and hearing by the Word of God. I have to hear the word from a man of God so faith can come to me. That goes for all of us. How can I hear and be taught the word without a pastor?" I thought that was very profound. He didn't say he was sitting under another pastor because he wanted to, but because the only way that faith could come was by hearing the Word of God from a man of God.

My dad asked me if I had an interest in boys. I didn't lie to him. I told him about Billy and how I found out that he was gonna ask me to the valentine's dance. He wasn't surprised. He just told me to be careful not to put myself in a vulnerable state.

We finished our dinner, and I helped my mother clean the kitchen. We had a nice time talking and getting revelation on the word of God. Those were the good old days. They always made sure their baby girl was spiritually ready for what life had to offer her.

"Ailina, come with me for a second dear," my mom said. I dried my hands off and followed her out the back door into the back yard. The sun was just beginning to set. We ended up in her garden. The garden was half the size of a one-bedroom apartment. She pulled up two chairs onto the patio area and told me to sit down. I sat next to her, and she started to stare into space.

"You want to show me something, mom?" I asked. She looked at me with a smile.

"This is my sanctuary. I come here to pray every morning. I pray in the spirit, and then I pray with my understanding. This is my place to dwell with the lord. I come here and set an atmosphere for him.

"What does that mean momma?"

"You mean praying in the spirit?"

"Yes." She took a deep breath and started to explain. I was all ears because I was curious. I never heard that before.

"The book of Jude in the New Testament tells us to build up our inner man by praying in an unknown language. It's called praying in tongues. We do this to be spiritually ready to fight against whatever is coming our way-things that we can't see. These things are in another realm. We are believers in Christ, there will be things coming our way to try to take that away. You want to hear something?"

"Yes," I said.

"I was in a meeting one day with boss. He made a decision that got me very upset. I didn't agree with it. So I gave him a piece of my mind. I went off on him so bad I almost said a curse word at him an got myself fired. If I had prayed that morning and had my inner man build up, I would have been spiritually ready to fight that battle." I was just listening to her and getting revelation on prayer. She explained everything I needed to hear about praying in the spirit. I caught on pretty quick. My mom and I started to do it together. We did that every morning. My dad had a little prayer closet he went into.

That night, I was in my room, putting on my nightclothes and getting ready for bed. I started going through my closet to pick out something to wear for school. There was a knock at my door, and it was my dad.

"Hi honey," he said.

"Hi dad."

"What time is that dance tomorrow?"

"It starts at five o'clock."

"What time is it over?"

"Eight."

"Okay, I'll be there to get you at exactly eight, okay?"

"Yes, sir. Thanks dad." I walked over to him and gave him a hug.

***

Sandra was actually right. At breakfast that morning, Billy really asked me to go with him to the dance. He seemed to be nervous and was stuttering like crazy. I told him yes, and we went together. Everyone was there. Toa, Sandra, Andrew, Billy, myself, and other friends. The DJ was playing fast music, slow music, old music, new music, etc. I saw Toa walking over to me. She looked like she wanted to ask me something.

"Come here for a second, chica," she said.

"What's up Gurl?" I asked.

"Let's go outside for a minute." We went outside and joined some friends. We were in the woods behind the school. It was almost dark. The students were kissing and feeling on one another. Right away, I knew something wasn't right. Billy joined us a moment later. He came over to me and tried to kiss me. I backed away from him and said,

"Billy, what are you doing?"

"What's the matter? Everyone else is doing it," he said.

"Yea, Li Li, don't you like him anyway?" Said Toa. I did like him, but at that point, something wasn't fitting to well in my spirit. I almost got sick to my stomach. Guys were putting their hands in girl's pants, grabbing their breasts, and kissing their necks. Billy tried to kiss me again, and I pushed him away.

"Billy, stop it!" I yelled. The other students stopped what they were doing and turned their attention on me. I could tell by the look on their faces that were getting very pissed off.

"What's the problem Li Li?" Toa asked.

"I can't do this, Toa I just can't." I looked at Billy and said, I'm sorry." Then I ran back into the school.

I went to the main office to use the phone. I called my parents to come and pick me up. I took heed of what my mother and father said to me at the dinner table. I wasn't gonna let any boy just degrade me like I was some kind of a tramp. Neither was I gonna let anyone touch my body because it is the temple of the holy spirit. They arrived moments later.

"Are you okay honey?" My mom asked.

"Yes, ma'am. I'm just ready to go home." I told them what happened. I didn't want to keep any secrets from my parents. They trusted me a lot, and I didn't want to lose that. I counted that as a blessing to be trusted by my parents the way they trust me.

"I'm very proud of you dear," my dad said.

Toa came to me the next morning at school when I was eating my breakfast. I guess she felt bad about the other night. She sat her tray down and sat next to me.

"Hi chica," she said softly.

"Hi."

"Listen, I'm sorry about the Valentine's dance. I wasn't trying to pressure you into doing something you didn't want to do. Please don't be mad at me." I turned and looked at her and said,

"You're my best friend, Toa I can't stay mad at you for long." She smiled at me and hugged me.

Billy didn't speak to me throughout the entire day. I didn't care though. The other students that were in the woods were just staring at me like they wanted to slap me.

***

I was in my last year of middle school. I was so excited because I was gonna be in high school soon. I wondered what kind of adventures awaited me now. What kind of classes would I be taking? Will I meet more friends? And what would my teachers be like? I couldn't wait. We were in the second semester of my last middle school year. My mom and I went into the prayer garden and gave thanks to our God before I went to school. She told me she and Dad would pick me up to get out for dinner. My grandparents were coming with us.

At the end of that school day, I walked Toa to her bus outside the school. I was waiting for my parents to come pick me up. We said bye to each other, and I went inside to wait for my parents. Ten minutes later, my principle, Principle Moore and two security guards walked up to me. They had a look on their faces that I would never forget. They looked as if they were coming to use me for a ritual sacrifice.

"Ailina, can you come with us to the main office please?" said Principal Moore.

"Sure." I followed them down the hallway, wondering what was going on. *Did I get in trouble? Did one of my friends get in trouble?* That wasn't even close.

"You may wanna sit down, Ms. Chauhan," said Principal Moore.

"Is there something wrong, sir?" I asked. Two officers came in. I had no clue what the heck was going on. They closed the door behind them. "Did I do something wrong, officers?" I was so scared. I didn't know what to do. One of them approached me and said,

"Hello Ailina. I'm officer Colwell and this is my partner, Officer Jones. We don't know how to tell you this but," he took a deep breath. "Your parents were in a car accident."

My eyes got big, and I put my hand up to my mouth, like was about to throw up. I started shaking.

"Please tell me they're okay, officers. Please tell me they're okay!" I yelled. They looked at each other and then back at me. I saw the same look on their faces that my dad had when he told me Mia didn't make it when she got hit. I jumped up off the chair and grabbed Officer Colwell by the shirt and just started yelling, "PLEASE… PLEASE… TELL ME THEY'RE OKAY, PLEASE!" I began to cry.

"We're very sorry ma'am," Officer Jones said. I dropped to the floor by the desk and screamed,

"NOOOOO, OH MY GOD NOOOOO!"

I couldn't believe it. Just like that, my mom and dad were gone. I had no idea what life had in store for me now. My parents were gone, and nothing was ever gonna make sense to me anymore. I wondered now, *What' next for me? First my childhood friend Mia, then my parents. This was too much for me to handle. How am I gonna serve God now?* What a turn of events this was.

***

There were more people at my parents' funeral than I thought there would be. It was hard for me to look at them in the casket like that. I sat next to my grandparents in the front row of the church. It was the saddest thing. I was just crying and crying until I was out of tears. I had no idea what was in store for me now that my mom and dad were gone.

It was time to view the bodies for the last time. When it was my turn, I stood over my dad for a while. I put my hand on his arm and said, "Thank you daddy, for always making sure I was okay. Thank you for being so proud of me. I love you daddy." I then walked to my mother's casket I said the same thing I said to my dad. After that, something took over me. I started to reach my hand in her casket. Then I just yelled out, "Get up mamma! Get up mamma, we have to go pray in the garden! Come on, mamma, get up! Get up! Get up! We have to go in the garden and pray, mamma, please... get up! My grandparents and my friends Sandra and Toa grabbed hold of me. Then I dropped to the floor and kept yelling and yelling.

I found out a semi-truck ran the red light an hit them. The car flipped over three times. I was grieving over my parents' death for a long time. I was sent to live with my grandparents. I never could get comfortable living with them. Not that I didn't want to be there, but it was because I couldn't look at no one else as my guardians but my mom and dad. My friends once told me that I wasn't the same. I stopped talking to a lot of people at school. I was still angry inside, angry that I wasn't gonna see my mother and father again and angry that I wasn't gonna hear my mom's words of wisdom.

I then lost control over myself. I became disobedient to my grandparents, my teachers, and anyone else who had authority over me. I was barely passing my classes. I started hanging out with the wrong group of people. I wasn't myself anymore. I wasn't no longer Li Li the good girl.

When I made it to the eleventh grade, things got worse. I started drinking and smoking marijuana. I would stay out late, and sometimes I never come home. My grandparents were talking about giving me away to the system.

"We don't know what else to do with you Ailina," my grandmother said. "We're trying our best to make sure you feel welcome and raise you the way your mom and dad would, but you're making that so hard for us child." I just blew it off and replied,

"I'm not making anything hard! Just stop trying to control me and let me be me!" I then stormed out of the living room and into my room then slammed the door. I turned my music on and sat on my bed. Then I buried my face in my pillow and cried. Living with my grandparents just wasn't the same as living with my mother and father. I didn't even try to get used to it. I was only used to being around my real parents and them only.

Some friends at school asked me if I would like to come over to their house. I quickly agreed. Toa, Sandra, and I went. There were boys there, other girls, and no parents. We smoked marijuana outside the house so that the house won't smell. Billy Rogers was there as well. We did all kinds of things-smoked, drank, danced to seductive music, etc. Billy was ignoring me. He wasn't staring at me but ignoring me still.

"I have an idea guys," said one of the girls. "Who wants to play truth or dare?" Everyone agreed.

We were daring people to do all kinds of things. Someone dared Toa to lift her shirt up and flash everyone. One girl was double dared to go in a closet with a boy for five minutes. They came out pulling up their pants and fixing their shirts. We knew they had sex in the closet. It was my turn. I wasn't scared at all. I was willing to be like the others and do what they did. "I dare you, Ailina to tongue-kiss Billy," Sandra said. I looked at Billy. He was sitting across from me in the circle. "Come on chica, he won't bite," she assured.

I'd never kissed anyone before. I decided to give it a shot. So I got on my hands and knees and slowly crawled toward him. My hair was hanging down, almost touching the carpet. I saw the look in his eyes that he was getting excited. I started teasing him even more by crawling slower. When I reached him, I placed my lips on his. Seconds later, I slipped him the tongue. I didn't do so bad for my first try.

I knew I wasn't supposed to be doing that. I knew I wasn't supposed to be at that house. I just stop caring about God's word because I didn't have my mom and dad to hold me accountable. The very two people who believed in me were gone anyway. So, I didn't care anymore.

"Dang chica, I didn't know you could do that," said Toa.

"I didn't either," I replied. One of the other girls said,

"That had to be the sexiest thing I've ever seen."

Billy was just smiling. He was probably thinking to himself, *finally, I got a kiss.* After the game truth or dare, we went outside to Billy's car. We were both inside smoking weed. I got really high and so did he.

"You kissed me like you've done that before," he said. I took a hit of the blunt, blew the smoke out, passed it to him and said,

"I know. Pretty impressive huh?"

"Yeah, I mean... that was amazing." I saw him looking at me up and down. I had on a skirt that was barely touching my knees. He then looked me in the eye and said, "Look, sorry for trying to throw myself on you at the Valentine's dance."

"That's okay." We both were high as ever. I felt the inside of the car spinning.

"Ailina, you used to be the good girl. What happened?"

"Let's not go there," I replied.

"Okay, forget I said anything. Can I ask you something?"

"Sure, go ahead." I sat up straight and fixed my eyes on him.

"Did you like that kiss as much as I did?" I turned my head toward the passenger window and looked out for a moment. Then I looked back at him.

"Yes... yes I did." He took another hit of the blunt and nodded as if he was satisfied with something.

"Will you get mad at me if I kissed you again?" he asked.

"Ummm... no, I don't think so." He then leaned over slowly and kissed me on the lips I grabbed his face and kissed him back. Next thing I knew, he was undressing me. I heard my mother's words going through my head over and over about boys. "don't let no boy degrade you." Then the sound of a car crash passed through my ears. So I just let him do whatever he wanted. I ended up having sex for the first time. When he put it in, it hurt for a little bit, then after a while, it felt good. I was making sounds I never made before. They were sounds I thought I couldn't make.

Toa and the other girls came over to the car moments after we were done. They were high just like we were. They were bragging on how they were having sex at the back of the house. They eventually put two and two together and figured out we did it in the car.

I knew my grandparents were gonna be mad at me for coming home so late. And on top of that, I was high as the sky off marijuana.

"Do you know what time it is child!" my grandmother said. She had her hands on her hips while tapping her foot on the floor.

"Yeah, its eleven o'clock." My grandpa came down the stairs. He had a really, really angry look on his face.

"Young lady, we were worried sick about you!" he said. "We almost called the cops and reported you missing!"

"I was just out with some friends. Don't get your panties in a bunch," I replied.

"At eleven O'clock at night Ailina!" my grandma said.

"Look, you don't have to worry about me. I can take care of myself, alright!"

"Listen here young one! You will not talk to us like that!" said my grandpa. "Now we took you in as our own to keep you from being in the system. The least you can do is show us some respect! Look at you, you're high as the birds. Have you been smoking?"

"What is that a crime?" I replied. My grandpa looked at my grandma and said,

"Should we tell her now? My heart sank. I was wondering what the heck they were talking about.

"Tell me what?" I asked.

"Your grandmother and I made the decision to give you to the state."

"What! I couldn't believe what I was hearing.

"I'm sorry child. But I have too many health problems as it is, and you're not making it any better. Ever since we took you in, my blood pressure been sky-high."

"You can't do this to me!" I yelled.

"We don't want to this, but we believe it will be best for your grandmother," my grandpa added.

I didn't know how to take that. I was so hurt I just wanted to fall out and die. The last thing I wanted to do was be an orphan child. I ran upstairs to the bathroom and slammed the door. I looked at myself in the mirror and started crying. I was no longer a good girl. I had sex for the first time, my mom and dad were gone, so I figured what is there to live for?

I opened the medicine cabinet and grabbed my grandmother's pills. I didn't remember how many I had in my hand, but it was almost a handful. I shoved them in my mouth and drank some water from the sink. My vision started getting blurry. Then my head started to hurt as if someone was inside, hitting my brain with a sledgehammer. It got darker and darker. Next thing I knew, I had hit the bathroom floor head first.

***

I tried to kill myself that night. I woke up in the hospital. The doctors had to pump my stomach. Apparently, I survived the suicide attempt. I felt woozy off the medicine they gave me. When I woke up, my grandmother was in the room with me. Never in a million years did I ever though that I would try to kill myself.

"How are you feeling, child?" my grandmother asked.

"Just tired," I replied. "How long have I been in here for?"

"Three days What were you thinking child? You could have killed yourself." The doctor came in moments later.

"How are you feeling Ailina?" she asked.

"I have a headache," I replied.

"I'll get you something for that." She left the room. My grandmother placed her hand on my forehead.

"You feel warm dear. You scared the living daylights out of me." I just kept quiet. Even talking made me feel woozy. The doctor came back in the room. She had a bottle of pills and a glass of water.

"Here, take two of these," she ordered. I sat up slowly and took the pills. My head was killing me. All throughout the day, doctors and nurses were doing tests and making sure I hadn't done any permanent damage to myself. Miraculously, I hadn't done permanent damage. I believed that was God for real.

The next day a counselor came in my room. He was an almost middle-aged Caucasian guy with a few gray strands of hair. He informed me that I wasn't gonna be able to go home until he felt that I was no longer dangerous to myself. I got mad as ever because I felt he had control over me. Nobody had control over me besides my mom and dad, not even my grandparents.

"Ms. Chauhan, I'm Tom Lander, one of the counselors at this hospital. It's my understanding that you tried to kill yourself by taking your grandmother's pills," he said. "Aren't you a little young to be going through midlife crisis?" I rolled my eyes at him and said with an attitude,

"And how do you know I'm going through midlife crisis??

"Well for one, you tried to kill yourself. Tell me something, what happened that made you want to do such a thing? I just wanna help you and get you home quick as possible."

"I'm not going into the system," I said.

"What do you mean?"

"I just got scared. That's all. Now can I go home?"

"It's not gonna be that easy my dear. What do you mean about going into the system?"

"I was threatened to be given to the state by my grandparents."

"Why would they do that?" I just started crying. He grabbed me some tissue off the counter.

"I'm a troubled teen! I hate my life! I FUCKING HATE MY LIFE!" I screamed.

"Whoa whoa whao," he said. "Calm down, sweetheart. Now we can get through this, and I'm gonna be right hear helping you. So, your grandparents threatened to give you up, and you decided to kill yourself?

"Yeah."

"Where's your mom and dad?" he asked. I began to cry harder. Then I told him what happened to them.

"I just wanna go home," I said. I want out of this place, now!"

"Not so fast dear, we still have quit a few steps to go through." I got mad. So, I grabbed the fork off my dinner tray and went for his throat. He caught my hand just in time before it penetrated him. I screamed over and over,

"GET ME OUT OF HERE! GET ME THE HELL OUT OF HERE!" I still had the fork to his neck, and he was hanging on for dear life. Then he started yelling,

"HELP ME! SOMEONE HELP!" Doctors and nurses ran into the room and grabbed me. One of them took the fork out of my hand. Then I started throwing punches at anybody and everybody I saw. Security came in and tried to restrain me. "Hold her down! hold her down!" said one of the doctors. The doctor walked over to me with a needle while I was held down on the bed. He poked me, and seconds later, it was lights out.

CHAPTER 3
The Lockdown

After that incident at the hospital, I was shipped to a psychiatric hospital forty-five minutes away from my grandparent's house. I hated that place worse that the medical center. They kept me in a cell most of the time because I was too violent. They kept me on drugs to make sure I stayed calm. I couldn't talk to my friends or go outside the gates. I was so miserable and lonely. I wanted out of that place so bad.

I was sitting on my bench in my cell one day, rocking back and forth. Then I heard the sound of keys rattling outside my door. One of the guards opened my cell. He had a tray of food in his hand. The guard was a very skinny guy. He wasn't all that tall either. His arms weren't that big, so I thought I could take him. "Here's your food Ailina," he said. I got up off the bench and slowly walked towards him. I took the tray from him, and he stared at me. He was looking at me like he wanted to throw himself on me. Then I slapped the tray in his face. The hot soup burned him, so he screamed as loud as ever. I ran out the open door and down the hallway. Seconds later, the alarm sounded. I heard a deep male voice over the intercom saying, "We have an escape in progress. This is not a drill. Please lock all the main doors." Obviously, the guard radioed to the base of the facility.

I kept running and running until I saw the exit to the outside. I tried to open the door I came to, but it was locked. I turned back around and ran down the other hallway. There was a guard coming around the corner. I didn't know what to do, so I ran as fast as I could and drop-kicked him in the stomach. He flew back at least five feet on the hard slippery marble floor. I tried the other door that was to the right of the hallway, but it wasn't budging. Suddenly, there were about six guards coming my way very fast. They had taser guns, pepper spray, and all kinds of things. I started running down the hallway some more as fast as I could. I felt my heart beating a million times per minute. I was so scared.

Suddenly I was running out of breath. I was slowing down. Finally, I was swooped off the ground, and a guard was on top of me, pinning me down. Then I was given a shot. I was out cold again.

When I woke up, I couldn't move. I was back in my cell on my bench bed. I finally realized that I was in a straitjacket. Just imagine that, a sixteen-your old girl in a straitjacket. I rolled off the bed and hit the floor. Part of me wanted to run my head into the wall until I died. I started yelling, "Let me out of here!" I was screaming out of anger.

They had me totally messed up, putting me in a straitjacket. Anger just took over my flesh, so I started kicking the door and screaming at the same time. The straitjacket was so tight on me I couldn't move a muscle. All I could move were my legs. I started banging my head against the steel door, trying to kill myself again. I banged my head so hard I got really dizzy and hit the floor. I was hoping I was dead. Two of the male guards came in and picked me up off the floor.

"Let me out of this jacket," I said. I couldn't yell because I caught a really bad headache from hitting my head. So, I whispered softly, "Please, let me out of this jacket."

"There, there now," said one of the guards. They sat me down and started unlocking the straitjacket. One of the guards went over to the door and closed it. Finally, I was free from the jacket. My head was bleeding from me hitting it against the door.

"I wanna go home," I said. I couldn't tell if it was day or night. Neither could I tell what time it was.

"You can't go home princess," said one of the guards. He took out a towel and wiped the blood off my forehead. Then he picked me up and sat me on the bed. Immediately I knew something was wrong. The guard then ran his fingers through my hair. I got so scared, wondering what the heck were they doing. Suddenly, I was grabbed by the throat. I couldn't scream or breathe. The guards then started to pull my clothes off. I got blindfolded with some kind of cloth. I was kicking and struggling to get free, but they were too strong for me. They spread my legs open, and I felt one of the guards inside of me. They took turns with me. I was so shocked and scared I couldn't scream or yell even if I tried.

When they were done, they put me back in the straitjacket and left the cell. I just laid on the bed in terror. My eyes were wide-open. I couldn't do anything but stand still as a statue. Mainly because I was so scared and shocked. The pain between my legs was excruciating. I began to shake. Tears came out my eyes. I slowly whispered the words, "Mommy, Daddy, where are you!"

***

The next day, I was still in shock. I didn't leave my cell to go outside or anything. I stayed in there all day. I didn't eat or anything, I didn't even want to take my medicine. They literally had to give me my medicine by force. I didn't tell anyone about the rape. They already thought I was crazy.

"No, no, no!" I yelled. "I don't wanna take these pills!" It took four nurses to give me my medicine.

"Calm down, ma'am, we just wanna give you your pills," said one of the nurses. I just kept screaming, until finally, they made the effort of giving me my medication. The medication made me woozy. Every time I took it, it was like I was in a twilight zone. It made me feel like I was the only person on this earth, waiting to die alone.

I was sitting on the bench in the recreation hall. Everything around me was black. My hearing was even off. My vision was going from black to white. Suddenly, stars begin to form. Then I started to see shadows of body movements. A familiar voice passed my ears. It was an old sweet type of voice.

"Ailina, Ailina, how are you feeling, dear? It was my grandmother. She sat down with me and rubbed my knee. "Ailina, can you hear me?" I heard her loud and clear but couldn't respond. That medication had me gone in the head. My eyes began to get very watery. I didn't even look at her because I was so drugged up. "Listen, my dear. I know you're mad at us for putting you in here. The quicker you get better, the quicker you can get out of here."

I had no idea that it was their decision to put me in this dump. And what the heck did she mean by get better? Well, I guess something really was wrong with me. I did try to kill myself and a counselor. The way I was feeling at that time was indescribable. I just wanted to get out of that place as soon as possible.

Suddenly, I started to nod off. My grandmother was still talking to me, but I could no longer make out what she was saying. She mumbled some words to me and hugged me. Then she left. I never saw how she looked that day because of the medicine.

Sharp pains began to develop around my pelvic area. That knocked me out of my little state I was in. The pain made me fall to the ground. Other patients were looking at me like what in the Sam Hill is wrong with her? The pain was a familiar feeling though. That was the same feeling I felt when I had my first menstrual cycle. Blood rushed down my legs like Niagara Falls. The nurses help me to the bathroom and gave me some sanitary napkins.

***

Months went by, I was making some kind of progress. I could have been out of there a long time ago. For some reason I kept trying to fight the other patients. Because of that, I had to stay longer because they felt like I was still a danger to others and myself. My anger build up when those two guys raped me. I later found out that one of the patients sliced their necks when they came to her room and tried to rape her again. They had been doing it to her for days. She stole a pocketknife from one of her visitors and hid it in her pants. When they came to her room, she sliced them up like a grain of wheat bread. They were dead instantly. I didn't know if they charged her with anything, but I do know she was transferred to another mental institution.

New patients were coming in, and old ones were making progress and leaving. I had to make some kind of progress so I could get out of this joint. I kept to myself and didn't socialize with anyone. It was time to take my medication, and three nurses came to my room. I hated that time of the day. This was my chance to try to make some progress. This was time to show them that I wasn't a threat anymore. So I submitted to them and calmly took my medicine. It tasted nasty, and the bitter aftertaste was even worse. They were shocked when I didn't put up much of a fight. "Good job Ms. Chauhan," said one of the female nurses. I kept doing that until they thought I was making enough progress to get normal room.

They moved me to a room and got me out of the cell I was in. Finally, I could see the sunshine and look outside and see the birds and the stars that glowed at night. They kept their eye on me though, making sure I wasn't trying to kill myself again. I had a shower in my room, a TV, and even a phone. My bed was twin-size.

The news was on, and I was eating my Jell-O with peaches in the middle. The news anchor lady was covering the story of two sisters who had been missing for months and were still missing. "Kayla and Matty have been missing for about four months now," said the news anchor. They showed a picture of them, and they were just the most beautiful girls. It was so sad for two young ladies to be missing like that. I hoped they would be found soon. The news anchor continued. "If anyone has any information on this case, you are asked to please call the tip line on your screen as soon as possible."

It was time to take my medication. The doctors had lowered the amount of dosage, considering the fact that I was making a lot of progress. So basically, the milligrams in my pills were lowered. I no longer got really drowsy when I took them.

"What are you watching Ailina," she asked.

"The news," I replied. She was a new nurse, and she was always so friendly.

"Your grandmother is coming to visit you real soon." My grandmother came in an hour later. I was sleepy because my medication was kicking in.

"Hello, dear, my grandmother said with a soft voice. I sat up on my bed and greeted her back with a smile. She sat at my bedside and ran her fingers through my hair. It was the same way my mother used to do it when I was sick or something. At that moment, my grandma reminded me of my mother. "Here, I brought you a piece of cheesecake that I made." She took out a container that she had in her huge red purse. I ate the cheesecake like I haven't eaten in days. I hadn't had cheesecake since my parents took me that nice restaurant downtown years ago. "I'm very proud of you, dear. You will be out of here pretty soon," she promised.

She brushed my hair, and we talked for a while. She was telling me the story on when she gave birth to my dad. "Your grandfather was trying to fight the doctors," she said. We both started laughing. Then she continued, "They had to kick him out of the delivery room until he calmed down. I was screaming and yelling, but I knew something beautiful was about to be born.

When they let your grandfather back in, I pushed your dad out three minutes later. My world lit up when I heard his cry for the first time."

I began to cry. I missed my father so much. I never saw my grandparents on my mother's side. They both went home to be with the lord when I was still a newborn baby. My mom never really talked about them as much. All I knew was that my grandfather from my mom side was a veteran in the armed forces and my grandmother from my mom's side was a stay-at-home wife.

***

I was allowed to do my schooling while I was in the psychiatric clinic so I wouldn't get so far behind. Tutors would come in and give me math and English lessons. I did a little experiment to see if I needed to my pills. Why did I do that? One time, they came in and gave me my pills, but I never took them. Instead, I spit them back out when the nurses left my room. So during recreation hour, I started to feel strange. I felt the urge to want to violently assault someone. I thought about when I was being raped, and something took over me. A man was walking past me, and I grabbed my butter knife off my tray and went after him. He saw me coming and ran off, screaming, "HELP... HELP SHE'S GONNA STAB ME!" Two security guards grabbed me and took the knife out of my hand. I was back in the cell.

I was only back the cell for a few hours. I admitted to them that I spit my pills back out and didn't really take them. They put me back in my room and told me not to ever do that again. That incident added more time to my stay. I was pissed off. Every time they gave me my medication, I had to open my mouth wide to show them that I took it.

I thought that was very ironic because I didn't get the outcome I wanted to get when I decided to skip out on my pills. Instead of not having a violent episode, I ended up actually having one. Definitely not the outcome I anticipated. During the recreation hour, the patients were avoiding me. They didn't come anywhere near me. I got the reputation of "you don't wanna be around her when she's off her medication."

My grandmother came to visit me again and told me she heard about my little violent episode.

"You can't be doing that, child, she said. "Don't you want to get out of here?" I started crying.

"Yes, yes I do."

"Well, you have to make sure you take your medication and stay out of trouble, darling. Okay?"

"Okay." For the first time, I felt like my grandmother really cared about me. It seemed as though she wanted me out of here just as much as I wanted out myself.

I was in my shower and heard my phone ring. By the time I stepped out and put my towel on, they had already hung up. I didn't know who called because I didn't have a caller ID. A nurse knocked on my door, and I permitted her to come in. "Time for your medication, darling," she said. I fixed my towel and took my medicine. I noticed the way she was looking at me. She was looking at me as if she liked what she saw. After I took my medicine, I cleared my thought and said,

"You can leave now!" she snapped out of her little fantasy world that she was in.

"Oh, yeah, sorry. Have a good day Ms. Chauhan." She stepped out and closed my door. My phone ranged again, and I answered it. I couldn't believe who it was. I was so happy to hear her voice I could have jumped up and down on my bed.

"Hey, chica!" It was my best friend Toa. I couldn't believe it. I hadn't talked to Toa since I tried to kill myself almost a year ago.

"Hey, Toa! Oh my God, how's my favorite chica!"

"I'm doing good gurl, I miss you. When are you getting out?"

"Soon, I hope. How did you know I was here?"

"Your grandmother told me. I was wondering what happened to you. I heard you went ballistic, gurl, trying to kill people." I took my towel off and put on some comfortable pajamas. Then I hopped in my bed.

"Whatever! What's new out there?" She started to tell me that Billy Rogers had moved out of town and that Sandra was still with Andrew. She just went on and on, catching me up on the world outside. I was saddened when I heard Billy had moved. I really liked him. Toa and I talked for a long time. I started crying to her, telling her that I wanted out of this place, and I wanted to see her. She agreed to come and visit me whenever she could.

We had talked on the phone at least once or twice a week for a month before Toa finally got around to come and visit me. I was so happy to see her. She walked into my room with her black hair curled up and blue jean pants. She had on a yellow short-sleeve T-shirt tucked in her pants. I hugged her tight as I could and cried on her shoulders. "I'm so glad to see you Toa." She started crying as well. We had a lot of fun in my room. She did my hair in curls with the curling iron I had in my bathroom. We talked and reminisced on the night I tongue kissed Billy Rogers.

Toa's visit that day pushed me harder to try and get out. I was on my best behavior. It got to the point where I was no longer antisocial. I said hi to people and always took my medication. I played board games with some of the patients. I tried so hard not to be so violent. I almost had a slip up when one of the female patients made a sexual statement towards me. I wanted to take my plastic spoon and shove it up her rear end. I wasn't allowed to have any sharp objects. Any eating utensils had to be plastic because of my violent temper.

The nurses and guards were noticing my behavior and gave a report to the state. They put in their report that I was fully matured and that I knew how to handle myself on my own and no longer needed to be there. They also said I was no longer a threat to myself or anyone else and felt that I was in good shape to leave the facility.

After that, someone from the state came out to evaluate me. My grandmother advised me advised to maintain my positive behavior and make a good impression. I was willing to do whatever it took to get me the heck out of this place. I kept a smile on my face. I didn't want to smile too much because I thought they would get the impression that I was trying to hard, and they would deny my release. I helped the nurses clean up after recreation hour and put away all the games. I made sure I took my medication for sure.

The lady from the state was very sweet. She was an African American lady with a gray pencil skirt on and a nice business shirt. She looked very professional. She had obviously read my case file because she went from detail to detail on how I first got put in this dump. She went from my parents' car crash to my suicide attempt and trying to kill other people. She was impressed with me and evaluated me for a week. Finally, she granted my application to go home.

I was happier than as squirrel with thousands of peanuts stored up for the winter. *What adventures awaits me when I go home? Can I do it? I mean. Can I make it without another violent episode?* I wasn't planning on having one, not unless I was physically provoked. I was planning on making sure I didn't put myself in that predicament. Curiosity flooded my flesh. *What's next for me? Am I ready? Or will I end up back in the slumber?*

CHAPTER 4
A Close Call

Free never felt so free. I was told to make sure to take my antidepression pills along with my other pills on the scheduled time. My grandparents picked me up from the facility. I was able to go back to school that following school year. I wasn't that far behind because I did some of my schooling in the joint in was in. I spent my whole eleventh-grade in the psychiatric hospital. My senior year came around, and more adventures were yet to come.

I was a totally different person in the twelfth grade. The goody - goody girl was no longer herself. Almost every school night, my friends and I hung out. We went to parties with guys and did things that could have gotten us in a lot of trouble. I stayed busy most of the time to keep my mind off my mom and dad. Every time I was alone in my room, I cried while looking at their picture sitting on my bed. That's why I hated being alone and by myself.

It was mid-night, and I got a phone call from Sandra. I knew something was going on because she never called me at that time. I got up and answered my phone. "what's up, chica?" I said,

"Hey, you feel like getting out again?"

"Right now?"

"Yeah, right now, your grandparents are sleeping, right?" I got out from under my covers and headed for the door.

"Hold on, let me see. They usually fall asleep at ten O'clock." I went downstairs and peeked inside their bedroom. Sure enough, they were asleep. "Yeah, they're sleep. What's going on?"

"Toa's parents are leaving for the weekend and she wants us to come over."

"Count me in," I said. I put on some attractive-looking clothes because I just knew boys were gonna be over. I went downstairs and slipped out the back door.

I made it to Toa's house, and it was just like I predicted. There weren't a whole lot of boys over but just enough. It was Sandra, Toa and me. There were only two boys. I had two drinks, and I was too through. Next thing you know, it went down. I'm talking about all kinds of things-sex, kissing, all you can imagine.

It was almost morning when I made it back home. I entered back in at the back door. Slowly I went to my room and laid down as if I had been there the whole night. Maybe they had been asleep and hadn't waken up to notice I was gone. I fell asleep around four O'clock in the morning. My grandpa woke me up around four hours later. It really felt like five minutes.

"Ailina, it's time for your medicine sweetheart," he said. I didn't feel like getting up, but I had to. I got up and took my medicine and went back to sleep. When I woke back up, it was almost one O'clock in the afternoon.

I called Toa to see if she was up but come to find out, she was up before me. She informed me that the gang decided to go to the movies in a little while. We all went, and I took my pills with me. That was ordered by my grandparents. We got off the bus at the transit station and walked the four minutes to the theater. "Toa hurry up slow poke," I said. She always walked so slow. "The movie starts in about twenty minutes."

"Here I come, dang! You don't have to rush me. I just saw a cut boy." She started laughing. Cars were passing us by and honking at us. It was rush hour and traffic was pretty heavy on Jane Lake Road.

We made it in time to catch our movie. The line was long, and I was getting mad. I always hated waiting in long lines. My alarm went off on my watch. I had set it at the time I needed to take my medicine. "Hold my spot in line guys," I said. "I have to go to the restroom really quick."

"Okay chica," Toa said. "We don't want you to go all crazy on us," teasing Ailina.

"Shut up chica," I replied with a laugh. I went to the restroom. When I got in there, I took my pills out of my purse and put two in my mouth and drank the water from my water bottle. The taste was still awful and bitter. I went back out and joined the gang.

The line had moved a lot since I was in the restroom. We brought our tickets and candy and went into the theater. We enjoyed our movie. An hour into it, I got a little light-headed. My medication was kicking in big time. After the movie, we walked back to the station. I was asked if I wanted to chill out over Toa's house. I told them no because I wasn't feeling good. "Oh yeah, your medicine is kicking in huh?" Sandra asked.

"Yeah, it is. Listen, I'll catch y'all later, okay?" I walked out of the station.

"Where are you going?" Toa asked.

"I'm about to catch this cab. See you! Love you!"

The cab ride made me feel worse. I got carsick. The cab driver was driving fast. Suddenly, the inside of the cab was spinning. I asked the cab to pull over. I got out and threw up on the sidewalk. "Are you okay?" the cab driver asked.

"Yeah, it's just my medicine I took." I got back in the cab, and he drove off. He drove slower and keep looking back at me to make sure I'm okay.

***

When I got home, I went to my room and laid down. I didn't feel like being bothered. My grandmother came in to see if I was alright. Man, I hated my medication. I hated the way it made me feel. I hated the taste. That was the first time I ever threw up afterward. "Hey Ailina, you alright, dear?"

"No, I feel dizzy. And my head hurts."

"Did you eat before taking your pills?" I thought about it for a minute. Well, that made sense. I should have eaten something. That's why I got sick.

"No, I guess I didn't."

"I'll make you some wild-rice soup," my grandmother said. She left the room. The soup was delicious. It made me feel better. All I needed was something in my stomach. I went out and sat with my grandparents in the living room. They were watching a Christian romance movie. I sat next to my grandmother.

"Looks like you're feeling better young one," said my grandpa.

"Yea, I am." After the movie, we all just talked, and my grandmother made chocolate chip cookies. They were delicious, especially with a glass of cold milk.

"You know Ailina, you look more like your mother to me," said my grandpa. "You have her eyes and her hair for sure."

"I tend to get that a lot," I replied. "I used to get that when they were alive. When my mom and dad went out to restaurants, people would come up to us and say, 'Oh, my, she looks just like you, Jan,'" I tried to change the topic because I felt myself about to cry. "So, grandpa, what kind of job did you used to do when you were younger?"

"Well, youngster, I was an auto mechanic. I loved working on cars. I was very good at it too. I'm still good at it though. I haven't worked on a car for quite some time now."

"That's how I met him, actually," my grandmother added. "My car caught a flat tire, and he just happened to pass me by and saw me. He fixed my flat tire for me, and we went on a date. Next thing I knew, we were married." I thought about that story for a minute. If my grandfather never took that road and fixed grandma's tire, I would have never been here. I had a nice time that night with them. I've learned that my grandmother used to be a head chef at all kinds of restaurants. That explained a lot with her great baking and cooking skills.

Later that night, I got a call from Toa. My heart just dropped again. She was crying and crying. I was trying to calm her down so she could tell me what happened. "What's wrong, Toa? Tell me what's wrong!"

"Li Li, I ca… ca… can't believe this shit!

"Toa, breathe for a minute, breathe and calmly tell me what happened," I heard her take a deep breath. And she started talking.

 "They followed us home."

"Who, who followed y'all?"

"Some random guys. We got off the bus, and three guys followed us."

"So what happened to Sandra?" is she alright? Did they hurt her?"

"She's in the hospital." My eyes got big.

"What the hell did they do to her!"

"One of the guys pulled out a knife and stabbed us. I'm fine though, but you know Sandra has a temper. She wasn't going for it." They got her pretty good. Sandra did have a temper, like the time she was about to fight Erica at the lunch table. I told Toa I was on my way to the hospital. I ran to my grandfather and told him the situation. He offered to take me to the hospital.

When we got there, I saw Sandra hooked up to machines. I ran to her bedside and grabbed her hand. Moments later, I cried. I lost one friend before; I didn't want to lose another. Andrew was there. Toa showed up with her parents. "Sandra, don't you dare die on me, chica!", I said. I knew she couldn't hear me. She was hooked up to breathing machines and everything. "Don't you even think about dying on me. Fight, girl, fight!" I remembered what my mother told me once before about prayer. I went to a corner and just prayed. "Father God, please don't take my friend away from me. Please let it be your will for her to survive this. Don't do this for me, God, but for her. I believe and receive, Father, what I'm praying to right now. Please, God, let her live." I then heard the sound that the heart monitor makes when the heart stops beating. *Beeeeeeeeeeeeeeeeeeep!* I ran over to the bed and yelled, "SANDRA, NOOOOOO!" The doctors ran in and tried to revive her. They ordered us out of the room. We could still hear the commotion from the outside.

"Clear!" they were shocking her heart to get it to start back up. "Clear!" said the doctor. I prayed again. Moments later, I heard a doctor say, "We have a pulse! We have a pulse!" Then the heart monitor machine started back up. They made the effort to revive her. The first thing I said was,

"Thank you, Father God! Thank you!" I got so scared. I thought I was gonna loose another person close to me.

***

That was a close one, a really close call. Till this day, I believed my prayer saved Sandra from leaving us that day. I didn't care what anybody said. God showed up because I called out to him. I didn't trust the doctors first, but I trusted that God would intervene and work through the doctors. I hoped Sandra got better before our senior prom. I was so happy it did turn out that way.

I went to visit Sandra in the hospital after school. Detectives took forensic samples off her from the scene including clothes fibers. Also, the knife used in the stabbing was found yards away from the scene. It had

Sandra's blood on it. They matched it to hers to be sure if that was the knife. They got a hit. They pulled fingerprints off Sandra's purses since it was leather. The robbers tried to snatch it from her. All three suspects had their fingerprints on Sandra's purse. The idiot didn't even think to wear loves. The fingerprints were submitted to the FBI criminal database and a hit. Immediately they arrested twenty-five-year-old Kevin James, eighteen-year-old Chris Matthews, and twenty-year-old Andre Loner.

Toa and Sandra were asked to look at some photos to see if they recognized them. They did very quickly. At the trial, all of them were charged with two counts of armed robbery since they took items from Toa and Sandra and first-degree attempted murder. The prosecution argued that the stabbing was an intent to kill.

The forensic evidence was too overwhelming for the defense. The clothes fiber matched Kevin James's clothes that were confiscated from his home. All three had their fingerprints on Sandra's purse. That alone pretty much put the nail in the coffin. The fingerprints on the knife were a match to twenty-five-year-old Kevin James. He was the ringleader. They had no alibis to give. they were found guilty of all charges. It was pretty much an open and shut case.

We were at the sentencing, and the judge really laid the hammer down on them. Their lawyers were trying to get the judge to give them ten years with probation after five years. The judge wasn't going for it. he started with eighteen-year-old Chis Matthews. "Mr. Matthews do you have any final words before I sentence you?" said Judge Cooper. Chris knew he was going away for a long time. I saw him cry. I didn't care if he cried a river. He deserved whatever the judge was about to give him. He turned to Sandra, who was in a wheelchair now, and said,

"Sorry about what happened to you. I wish I could take it back."

"Mr. Matthews, for the charges you've been found guilty of, this court hereby sentences you to thirty years in the state penitentiary. You'll be eligible parole after you've served seventeen years." He dropped to the floor hard. The court marshals. Snatched him up. The judge then got to Twenty-year-old Andre Loner. "Mr. Loner, any last words?" He didn't even look at Sandra.

"The only thing I can say sir, is sorry for my actions." I saw the look on the judge's face. I could tell he was disgusted.

"Mr. Loner, you're hereby sentenced to thirty years." Your eligibility for probation will be after seventeen years. He was snatched up the marshals. Finally, he got to the sick bastard who almost took Sandra's life, Twenty-five-year-old Kevin James. Mr. James, what do you have to say for yourself for committing such a horrible crime?" He shrugged his shoulders and said,

"I just needed money."

"What did you need money for?" Judge Cooper asked.

"Drugs." I was thinking, at lease he was honest.

"Mr. James, you have been arrested for battery, drug distribution, burglary, and the list goes on and on. You violated your probation while committing these crimes. It doesn't look so good for you, my friend." Kevin James smiled. I couldn't believe he thought this was funny. "You find this funny Mr. James!"

"Nope.' He replied.

"Now, Mr. James, since you violated your probation and you're the one who tried to kill this young lady, There's a lot of aggravating factors in this case. You're hereby sentenced to life in the state correctional facility. You'll be eligible for parole after at least thirty-five years on top of that you will serve out the remainder of probation in prison." He was snatched up by the marshals.

***

Sandra was going through physical therapy so she could learn to walk again. I felt bad for her for having to go through a near death experience by some jerks who just wanted money. I knew how it was having a near death experience. She was coming along quite well. She broke the news to me that Andrew asked to marry her after high school. We talked over the phone.

"Oh my God, did he really!" I asked.

"Yes, he did."

"Can I be one of your bride's maids?"

"Now you know you and Toa are my two favorite chicas."

"Yayyyyyyyy!" I yelled.

"Ailina, I have to tell you something." I sat up on my bed and said, "What's up?"

"I died that day." I figured that when the machine went blank.

"I know, it scared the hell outta me."

"No, you don't understand. I died to my flesh." I remember hearing that from my dad. He once told me that in order to follow the Lord Christ, we have to die to ourselves. That means to now give up the old way of thinking, deny what we think is right, and take up what God thinks is right. This was some serious stuff.

"So, what are you saying? You're turning your life around?"

"Yes, yes, I am. When I died, I heard the Lord say he'll give me life if I submit myself to his will, his word, and his way of doing things. I promised I would if he didn't let me die."

"Wow, that's deep," I said.

"Li, there's something else I want to tell you. I don't know what to make of this, but God wants me to tell you something. I hope it's not too late."

"What's that?"

"He said to tell you to follow the man who reaches his hand out for you. He said something remarkable will happen when you do." Honestly, I didn't know what to make of that either. For some reason, I held on to it. I believed her. I had no idea what God meant by that.

***

Prom night rolled around, and Sandra was healed just in time to go with her fiancé. We all had prom dates, and things were okay. I made sure I took all of my medications. I also made sure I ate first. I got sick last time. We had fun dancing and eating great food. The punch was also good. We had on the same color dresses. I always loved dresses. We had on ruby-red-color strapless dresses that came down to the floor. I thanked my grandparents for buying it for me. Our hair was done the same way. My hair took forever to get done because it was the longest. We all got a nice wash and then curls-our favorite type of hairstyle. People used to say we acted like sisters.

The gymnasium was decorated so wonderfully. The tables had white cloths on them with breathtaking centerpieces and balloons pinned down in the center of the table. Colorful ribbons were hanging from the ceiling with disco balls like we were back in the '70s.

I was sitting down drinking my punch, when my prom date asked me If I wanted to dance. I got up and joined him on the dance floor. The music was fast, so we danced fast. Then the DJ got on the mic and said, "Okay, Okay, we gone slow it down for y'all right now. So, if you have your prom date with you, grab'em by then hand and pull'em over to the dance flo." A slow song came on, and my date pulled me close to him. I could smell his cologne when it hit my nose. It smelled good. He put his hands around my waist, and I wrapped my arms around his shoulders. I looked over and saw Toa with her date, and to my other side, I saw Sandra with her future husband. We all were dancing slowly to the music.

***

After the prom, we went to hotels of course, there were sex involved. The only two who didn't do it was Sandra and her fiancé because she said she was doing right by God for saving her life. Her fiancé Andrew was all right with that. Sandra was serious. I was proud of that. My prom date could have got some that night, but the way he went for it was unacceptable.

"Okay sweetness, here we are," he said. He started taking off his clothes.

"What are you doing?" I asked.

"What do you mean? It's about to happen. You already know what it is." I was disgusted.

"Ummm, why can't it be more romantic?"

"This is prom night baby." He moved closer to me. I stepped back.

"Listen, I don't feel right about this. I mean, let's take our time and flow with the moment." He wasn't trying to hear that.

"Naw, girl, I'm ready now." He then tried to kiss me on my lips. Okay, he better relax. He doesn't know me. I can get dangerous. He must not know my background.

"Come on, baby. What's the problem? We gonna do this or what?"

"I told you what the problem is. You're not making me comfortable enough." He tried to kiss me again, and I pushed him back. Then he grabbed my butt. That was the last straw. I kicked him in his man parts, and he fell to the floor screaming. "Keep it in your pants tonight. My friend," I said. Then I left out of the hotel room. My grandparents picked me up, and I went home.

***

Graduation came around, and we walked across the stage to receive our diplomas. It was an awesome ceremony. My grandparents supported me by being there. It was a beautiful day in June. Students were giving speeches, and teachers were congratulating student. I cried. I cried hard because my mom and dad couldn't live long enough to see this day come. Toa and Sandra came over and held me when they saw I was crying. Sandra got married to Andrew, and Toa and I were here bride's maids. Her sister was her maid of honor.

Toa and Sandra, both told me that they were attending college out of state. I got so sad and heartbroken. We made sure we stayed in contact with one another. They left after the summer ended. We hung out that whole day before they left. We went to the mall and shopped. It was sad to see them leave. They both ended the night over my house to say goodbye to me. "We gone miss you chica," Toa said. Then she gave me the biggest hug. Sandra came over and said,

This is not goodbye. We will visit every summer break." She took off her favorite tennis bracelet and gave it to me. "Here, keep this for me." She placed it around my wrist. We all cried, and they both said, "Bye chica." I wiped my eyes and replied,

"Bye chicas." Then they left.

Toa and Sandra are the closes family I have besides my grandparents, especially Toa. We had known each other since kindergarten. She and I go way back.

Well, what is next for me? My two best friends were gone. I wasn't planning on going to college until I could get off these pills. I wanted to be a fashion designer. Time went by so fast. It was time to get myself together. But first, I had to get better. I was suffering from depression and Anxiety. My mental state was so unbalanced the slightest thing could set me off on a negative rampage. I knew my grandparents weren't going to be around forever. It was time to make something happen. And man, did I make the most crucial decision ever that would come back literally to hunt me in the future.

CHAPTER 5
God Please Help

I tried to maintain a positive relationship with my grandparents. I just knew there would be a time when I was going to need them again. When Sandra and Toa left, my grandparents did what they could to comfort me. I tried my hardest to get off those pills. I wanted better for myself, but I knew I needed help. Someone was gonna have to help me.

I got a full-time job as a waitress at a restaurant. I got the job so I can have some money. My Boss made it perfectly clear to me that I needed to take my medication on time and not to miss one appointment. I really felt like those pills were controlling me. It made me angry every time I had to take'em. It also made me feel embarrassed. People always looked at me like I just drunk out of the toilet when they saw me in the bathroom taking my pills at work. One time, I just went inside the stool in the woman's restroom and cried. I was on my break.

The first month working there was okay. I was doing quite well. I loved meeting new customers and making sure they were having a nice time at the restaurant. I would chat with the kids who came there with their parents and play with the babies. "How does every taste, guys?" I asked one of the families at a booth.

"Everything is fine, ma'am. Thank you, said the father. They were a nice family. I've learned that it was one of the kids' birthdays. The little girl turned ten, and they were out celebrating. She reminded me of my childhood friend Mia.

I ended my shift one evening and walked to the bus stop to go home. It was pretty hot. So, I took off one of my shirts. I had a T-shirt on under my long-sleeve sweatshirt. A two-door all-black car rode up to me. It was occupied by a gentleman who looked like he was in his early to mid-thirties. He wasn't bad looking, and his skin was a shade darker than mine. His name was C-Lo. I should have known by the name that he wasn't the one for me and up to no good. He asked me for my number, and I gave it to him.

C-Lo called me that night. His voice sounded deeper over the phone than it did in person. We talked and dated for months, and everything seemed to be fine. He asked me to move in with him. The first time I said no because it was too soon. I talked to my grandparents about it. I knew they were right when they said it was a horrible idea. but I just wanted something different. I thought maybe he could help me get off these pills and help me find my true self. "Ailina, have you gone mad child?" my grandmother said. "You don't know that man from the hair on his head to the bottom of his feet. On top of that, you shouldn't be laid up with a man that you're not married to. That's not the plan God has for you. Your mom and dad taught you better than that, Ailina, I just know they did."

"Grandma, you know I hate it when you bring up my parents," I said in a calm tone voice.

"She's just trying to make a point. Li Li," said my grandpa. "That man has no intentions on marrying you. Even if he does, he isn't saved. He doesn't even know the Lord." I knew they were right. I tried my luck anyway. I was being stubborn.

"What do you want me to do, live here until I die?" I asked sarcastically.

"You can live here as long as you need to dear," my grandma said. "It's a dangerous world out there, and we gonna be here to protect you from it."

"Thanks Grandma, but I can manage just fine. I'm nineteen years old, and I can handle myself."

"Are you stupid, or just playing stupid!" my grandpa said, with a look of aggravation on his face.

"Don't call me that!" I yelled.

"I Didn't call you anything, I asked a question. You can take it how you want it. Now are you stupid or just playing stupid!" that pissed me off very badly. I stared at him with the meanest glare. I stared at him as if he called me a bitch. I stormed to my room and packed my bags. Then I called C-Lo. He came and picked me up. Little did I knew; I was in for a wild walk on the wild side.

***

So I moved in with C-Lo, and for a while, things were going just fine. He was a drug dealer and was always drinking. He got drunk every opportunity he gets. He wasn't the romantic type either. He snapped when I mentioned marriage. He said he would never get married because that's not him. He started to become abusive when he got drunk. He began to be very controlling. Every time I went to pick up my medication from the pharmacy, he would think I was meeting another guy. Things were all bad for me, and I was in a situation I couldn't get out of by myself. When it came to making money, he made sure I was part of the act. I thought moving in with him would unlock the key to getting free from these pills, but later on, I found out that my condition was worse because of him. More stressed and depressed than I've ever been. When I bought that to his attention, he got offended and slapped me. "If you ever, and I mean ever, come at me like that again, I will make sure that you're more than depressed!"

I got scared of him. He was so intimidating that I was scared to even walk pass him. He would get mad if I didn't want to smoke weed or drink liquor with him. I would do it so he wouldn't beat me. One morning, I was taking my medication and getting ready for the day. I had the day off work. C-Lo came in the bath room and asked me to do a drug run with him. "I don't know C. I don't want to be a part of that," I said. I didn't see myself as a drug dealer. When I told him no, it was like I told him he had a disease he couldn't get rid of. When I was putting my medicine back in the cabinet, he used both hands to grab me by the throat. The grip was so tight I thought my eyes were gonna pop out my sockets. Then he said,

"Listen, bitch, you do what I say and when I say it! There is no telling me no! Did I make that clear enough!" he let go of the grip when he started to notice I was about to pass out. I held my throat while I gasped for air. So I just went with him.

C-Lo came home drunk one day, just minutes after I finished my shift. It was obvious that he had been with another female. He had hickeys on his neck, and his breath smelled like a woman's private area. I wasn't surprised at all. I finally had a reason to leave him. At least I thought I did. "C-Lo, have you been with another woman?" I asked. He couldn't really respond because he was so drunk. He didn't know whether he was coming or going. "C-Lo, I can't do this with you anymore, I just can't do it."

"What are you saying Ailina, Huh?"

"I'm saying I want out of this relationship." Why did I say that? He got up off the couch and walked toward me. I took a few steps back in terror. He slapped me so hard I flew over the coffee table. My nose was bleeding, and my face was red as an apple. *"No, C-Lo, please Noooo!"* I yelled. He picked me up by my hair and slapped me again. This time, I hit the wall and fell to the floor. I screamed as if I was being tortured with a taser or something. I was kicked and punched numerous times, and I thought he was gonna kill me that day.

"You will never leave me," he said. "The last females the left me, it wasn't good." All I could do was just lay on the floor in a fetus position, wishing I had listened to my grandparents.

He beat me so bad; I couldn't go to work the next day. I had to get out of this relationship soon before I got killed. I just knew there was something better for me. I knew I didn't deserve the way I was being treated. I thought I was too beautiful and worth more to be used as a punching bag. I was too beautiful to be letting someone mess up my pretty face.

Things got worse. He decided to take things to the extreme. He made me quite my job and kept me hostage in the house. I feared for my life. How the heck was I gonna get out of this? Only God knew.

***

So, the maniac decided to put bars on the windows and locks on the doors. He kept me in the room for hours a day. I came out only to use the bathroom, take a shower, and take my medication. I was so depressed, scared, bitter, and all other negative words you could think of. I wanted to kill myself so bad.

C-Lo came into the room one day with a proposal. It was more like a demand. I knew I had no choice in the matter. He just made it seem like I had a choice, but I knew he was full of crap. "I have an idea to make some money." What he meant was he knew how to make some money for him and him only. I was sitting on the bed with my red gown on. First, he told me take a shower and to my hair real nice. Then he wanted me to put on some make-up. I didn't know what the heck he had in mind. I just knew he was up to no good. Moments later, two buddies of his showed up. I just knew something wasn't right. "I want you to have a threesome with these guys here," he said.

"C-Lo are you fucking kidding me!" I couldn't believe it. he wanted me to let two strangers run a train on me. "I don't think I want to do this. C-Lo, please don't make me do this I'm really not up to that." He closed the room door and grabbed me by the throat and said,

"Listen here. Little princess. I have a lot of money riding on this, and if you don't comply, I won't get paid. Understand?" he let me go, and I said,

"Yes, I'll do it."

"Good," he said. Then he left the room.

I was looking stupid, as if I was lost somewhere. The two guys came in and closed the door behind them. They started taking off their clothes and smiling at me. One of the guys began to kiss me on my lips. I was trying not to kiss him back. But I just had to go with it so I wouldn't get beaten again. I was forced to perform oral sex on them. I just felt like a dirty whore. I felt like a hoe. In my mind, I just tried to find some sort of comfort by thinking to myself, *I'm only doing this by force.* They undressed me and took turns going in and out of me. I was forced to perform oral sex on one guy while the other guy did me from behind. The moans from my mouth were loud as ever. I just kept thinking to myself, *this isn't me… this isn't me.*

When they were done with me, I took a shower. I was scrubbing myself with my towel and crying at the same time. I was scrubbing so hard I thought I was gonna scrub the skin complexion off of me. The tears were just flowing down my face, along with the water from the shower head. I was so humiliated and degraded. I never thought my life would turnout like this. I missed my mother and father so much. I looked at myself in the mirror and thought this was it for me. It was not gonna get any better than this.

I was locked back up in the room. I felt like I was back in the mental institution. I was miserable. I wanted to just die. Ironic as this might seem, I wasn't his girlfriend at all. I was just a tool that he could make money with, just a tool that he could use for his sexual pleasure and make money.

The affair continued. He would let all kinds of guys pay him to have sex with me. It was to the point where I felt that I had to get high and drunk just to get into it. C-Lo had one guy come over to have his way with me. I guess C-Lo needed some money to pay the light bill. I was so drunk that I passed out on the couch in the living room. He and his friend had their way with me while I was passed out. I could feel the motion, and I could feel me being tossed and turned over and over. I couldn't moan at all. Getting drunk was my way of not having to see me get treated like a slut. I didn't want to be sober at all.

***

I needed God to just somehow come and intervene and make this situation go away. So, I did what my mom and I used to do in the garden-pray. I prayed for forgiveness. I admitted that I was wrong for treating my grandparents the way I did. At least it was a start. I didn't know what else to do. My mother once told me to never fight a spiritual battle in the flesh. She said, "The battle is not ours, but God's."

Honestly, I'd rather be back at the mental institution than to be in this place. I was actually held hostage. Another one of his guys came over. But this one was different. This guy wasn't like the others. I overheard them talking in the living room. C-Lo was trying to get him to pay for sex. "C-Lo, you owe me for the car. I need my money and I need it now!" the guy said.

"I don't have it now," C-Lo replied. "Look, I have something else for you. I'll let you have sex with my woman in there to pay off the debt. She's pretty too. we can call it even."

"Excuse me. You know that's not the kind of person I am. I don't sleep with random women. I just want my money C, and I want now, or I'll see you in court.

"Okay fine, take your money! Moment later I heard the door close. I was glad he didn't want to do it. He seemed like the kind of guy who respects women.

C-Lo stormed in the room pissed off. He took his anger out on me. So, he slapped me and threw me on the bed. Then he snatched my clothes off and stuck his penis in me. When he was done, he locked the door again and left. My vagina was hurting after that. It felt like I was bleeding. I put my clothes back on and grabbed a cigarette off the dresser. Tears just flowed down my face as I lit it up and put it to my mouth. My hands were shaking as if I was having a seizure. I fell asleep and woke up to find C-Lo standing over me. I jumped up and leaned my back against the headboard. I thought he was gonna beat me again. He asked me-well, made me, get up and clean the house. The house was so jacked up it looked like some college students had had a party in their dorm room. It took me about three hours to clean the whole place.

Even though I wanted to just die, part of me wanted to find out what was next for me. The next day, another buddy of his came over. It didn't take a rocket scientist to figure out what he came over for. I couldn't believe he actually made a living off selling my body to other men. He would charge almost any random guy that wanted to have sex with me. The range were anywhere from two hundred to five hundred dollars depending how long they wanted me for.

His boy came into the room, and I was already naked. His eyes got big when he saw me laying in the bed with no clothes on. He had his way with me for an hour and left. I got used to the whole thing. No longer did I cry afterwards. If I could turn back the hands of time, I would have listened to my grandparents. An opportunity had to come for me to get out of this dreaded, scary, and depressing chapter, and by the grace of God, I've found one.

I was forced to do another drug run with C-Lo, and crazy as it might seem, I was happy. This was a time for me to formulate a plan to escape. The perfect idea came to me. With this plan, I had to be quick. The whole thing went according to plan. He made me get drunk with him and smoke some weed, which was not part of the plan at all. I had to be sober, but I figured I could still pull it off.

First, I had to pick an argument with him. I figured doing that would knock him off his guard. I had to do it while he was driving in order for this to work. The drug run location was somewhere just a few blocks from downtown. He said he had a pound of marijuana to deliver. That was even better because what I was gonna do, involved the car being searched by police. So, I put my plan into action. "I thought you were a great guy when I first saw you, C.", I said. He turned and looked at me. Then he smiled. "What are you smiling about? I'm serious."

"I am a great guy, I'm a genius," he replied.

"You're an asshole if you ask me." The look on his face was scary. He looked like he wanted to pull the car over and beat the daylights out of me.

"Don't forget who you're in the car with, you dumb bitch!"

"I know exactly who I'm in the car with. A low-life coward who can't seem to grow up and develop as a man." Now remember, I was already drunk as a skunk.

"You want me to pull this car over and fuck you up!"

"You don't need to. I'll do it for you." I grabbed the stirring wheel and turned it hard as I could to the right. The car crashed into someone's yard and knocked down their fence. C-Lo hit his head on the steering wheel, and amazingly, I was unharmed. I got out of the car and ran as fast as I could. I ran until I couldn't run anymore. I hopped on a bus that was headed towards my grandparents' house. The idea was to go back to my grandparents. I was surprised when I made it there.

I knocked on the door and got no answer. I rang the doorbell, and there was still no answer. When I peeked in through the window, I noticed that all the furniture was gone. It appeared that they had moved, and I had no idea where they had moved too.

***

Now where was I gonna go? If it wasn't one thing, it was another. My phone had been taken by that jerk, and I didn't have any change to call my grandmother's cell phone. I didn't care what happened to C-Lo and neither did I wanted to find out. All I wanted to do was get the hell away from him. This was one of the loneliest times I've ever felt. So, I walked and walked, and it got dark. It was like I was walking through a town located in another country. I came to a bridge, and I ran toward it. I climbed on top of the ledge and contemplated on if I should jump.

There was nothing for me to live for anyway. My parents were gone. My grandparents were MIA. My two best friends were away at college. So, I leaned over to jump. I was breathing very hard. My heart was beating a million times per minute, and I was sweating. My feet started to slip, and I caught my balance. I held on to the rails, looking down at the river. I looked down to my death that awaited me. I felt even more drunk than I was earlier. I counted to three in my head. I was about to let go of the rail. *One, two…*

51

CHAPTER 6
Courtney

Right when I was about to jump, a set of headlights were approaching me. I didn't want to turn around to see who it was because I thought it was the police. The sound of screeching tires passed my ears. I noticed that it wasn't the cops because I didn't see any red or blue flashing lights. Neither did I hear any sirens. The car stopped. Someone got out. Then I heard the car door slam shut. I was still looking down at the river, breathing hard and drunk as ever. Footsteps approached me. "Whoa, whoa, whoa! Hold on there, sweetheart. Just hold on for one second. You don't wanna do that," a male voice said. It wasn't a deep voice but wasn't very soft either. The voice sounded familiar as if I heard it before. I didn't turn around to look at him right away. Then he continued. "Come on, my dear, please get down from there. I don't know what you're going through, but it isn't worth killing yourself, honey."

I slowly, slowly turned to look at him, still breathing hard as ever. He was average height and medium build with short curly hair. He looked very handsome. He started to walk toward me. "Stay back," I yelled. "Or… or I'll jump! I mean it!" he put his hand up as if I had a gun on him, and he stepped back saying,

"Okay, okay, no problem. I don't want you to jump." Then I screamed,

"What do you want from me! You wanna have your way with me too! Did that jerk send you to *fuck* me for money too! Why does everybody wanna fuck me, Huh!" Is that all you men want from me! To use my body, fuck me until I can't walk anymore!" I was just saying anything that came to my head out of frustration. I was totally wasted. He had a look of confusion on his face.

"No my dear, not at all. I'm not that kind of person. I just wanna help you. You don't have to do this."

"Well, you can't help me! You can't cure me." Tears were in my eyes. "I'm too mentally unbalanced."

"Maybe I can't, but I know who can." Now who did he know that could possibly help me? Then he said,

"God can." I didn't know how to respond to that. I had no comeback at all. So, I was silent. "Can I just talk to you for a minute? Please don't jump. Hear me out first." I looked him in the eye and said,

"I'm listening."

"First of all, my name is Courtney. May I know yours?" He sounded so proper when he said that. Such an innocent, sweet voice. He also sounded like he really didn't want me to jump.

"Ailina, my name is Ailina."

"Hi Ailina."

"Hi." I was getting a little calm. I wasn't shaking or breathing hard anymore. Maybe that was a part of his plan- to introduce himself and take the focus away from me wanting to jump. It worked like a charm because I was calmer than an old lady sitting in a rocking chair.

"I know why you're trying to kill yourself." *Yea right,* I thought to myself. But I was wrong. What he said next was a hundred percent true. I knew it was.

"You can't see no other way to fight your battle, and you're at your breaking point." His voice got softer. I think it was because he didn't want to sound intimidating. Then he continued. "It seems as though you can't figure out how you're gonna come of whatever situation you're in." I started crying. "I don't know what you're going through or what happened, but trust me, it's not worth doing this to yourself. Listen my dear, sometimes we just have to step out of the way and let God be God in our lives. Let the holy spirit take over and things can never go wrong. Trust me."

"Are you a pastor or something?" I asked.

"No, just a church boy, if that's what you wanna call it." I kind of smiled a little.

"Aye, you smiled. That's a start." That was the first time I had smiled in ages. He talked to me for a long time, being very sincere and considerate. "listen sweetheart, I know I haven't known you for that long, but I really, really don't want you to jump. Do you have kids?"

"No."

"A husband?"

"No."

"So, if you ever want them, how would you know if you will ever have a family of your own if you killed yourself?" If you do this to yourself, you will never see the power of God. Don't you want me married, have kids, a wonderful family, nice house, a church family or anything like that?" I cried again. He was right. I did want that. I longed for it, but I just never knew how to go after it. he read me like a book. It was like he knew me. I looked at him and yelled,

"What should I do right now! My mind is stuck on stupid! Look at me! I'm standing on the edge of a bridge drunk, about to kill myself! How do I go after what I want in life? I don't know what to do right now! What should I do!" More tears flowed. He slowly reached out his hand to me and said,

"Give me your hand." I immediately remembered what Sandra said to me on the phone before she left for college. She told me that God said for me to follow the man who would reach out his hand to me. This was what he meant. God knew this was gonna happen. He knew I was gonna try to kill myself again. He sent Courtney my way to save me. My heart felt like it was gonna burst out of my chest. My eyes widened. It was the most powerful thing I'd ever encountered. There was a brush of adrenaline. Courtney walked slowly towards me again, taking baby steps as if he was afraid that I was gonna jump if he got to close. Please darling, please take my hand. I can help you find God."

He finally made it to the ledge, standing behind me. So I reached out my hand to him. He grabbed it. his hands were so soft and smooth. "That's it, dear. Step down, nice and slow. I won't let you fall." When I turned around to step down, my left foot slipped off the edge. Courtney grabbed my right arm just in time. I was dangling off the bridge while he held my arm with both of his hands.

"PLEASE, DON'T LET ME FALL COURTNEY! I CHANGE MY MIND! I DON'T WANNA KILL MYSELF ANYMORE!" I yelled.

"I got you. I won't let you go, just stop wiggling so I can pull you up!" I kept wiggling. "COURTNEY, I'M SLIPPING! PLEASE DON'T LET ME GO! I felt his hands losing grip very slowly. Then he said very calmly, but loudly,

"Ailina, listen to me! You have to stop wiggling! You're making my hand slip and I can't pull you up!" I stopped wiggling. He was able to tighten his grip on my arm. He pulled me up, and my bottom was on the ledge. He wrapped his arms around me and pulled me off the edge. When I reached the ground, I passed out in his arms from exhaustion and drunkenness.

***

God really showed up that night. I could have been dead today. It was always a mystery to me on how God works until I realize that it's always his plan for his people to succeed for the sake of him. I woke up the next morning with a headache. I had no idea where I was. The smell of beacon hit my nose. I heard some food frying on a stove. My eyes were blurry, and they took a while to get used to the light. It was obvious that I had a hangover.

I realized that I was in a bedroom when I saw dresser drawers and closet doors. I sat up quickly and threw the covers off of me to see if I still had my clothes. I had on clothes, but they didn't look like mine. Somehow, I ended up in female pajama bottoms and a T-shirt. I noticed I didn't have on any underwear. I put my hand on my temple because my head was just killing me. I had no idea where I was. Moments later, a familiar looking face looked into the room. "Oh, you're finally up," how are you feeling?" It was Courtney. I went ballistic in the room.

"WHAT DID YOU DO TO ME! DID YOU RAPE ME! WHERE THE HELL AM I!"

"Relax. It's okay. Everything is fine. I didn't do any such thing. You just passed out in my arms last night. I didn't know where to take you, so I brought you to my apartment. I saved your life on the bridge last night, remember?" Now that it was daytime, Courtney looked even more handsome than he looked on the bridge, sexy as hell.

"Where are my own clothes?"

"Oh, I have them in the washer. You threw up all over them, and… ummm… you also urinated on yourself." I was so embarrassed "I put you in the tub and washed you up really good while you were out of it. your bodily fluids were all over me." He smiled. You would think he would have taken me to detox. This guy actually took the time out to bring me to his home, wash me up, and wash my clothes.

"So, you saw me naked?" I said, sarcastically.

"Well… yea… but I wasn't lusting after you or anything like that. I was just taking care of you, just as if you were a baby. I'm not that kind of person." I looked at him like, *yea right. You know you liked what you saw.* "What, I'm serious. I wasn't looking at you like that while I was washing you, are you hungry? I have some breakfast cooking."

I was hungry, and my head was pounding. "Ummm, sure. I think I have a hangover. My head is really killing me."

"I have something for that," he replied. He went in the bathroom and came back with a pill bottle and a glass of water. "Take these. It will help with the headache." It reminded me that I had to take my medication, but I didn't have them with me anyway. I took the pills and drank the water. They worked like a charm.

He came back in the room with a tray of food. It was eggs bacon, sausage, waffles with syrup and grape jelly, grits and some orange juice. I couldn't believe he brought me breakfast in bed. The food was delicious. I chowed down like I haven' eaten in days. "I'm gonna go check on your clothes," he said. Minutes later, he came back with my clothes. His bathroom was really clean. He gave me a toothbrush so I could brush my teeth. I put my clothes on an joined him in the living room.

"You can have a seat if you'd like." I sat down on the couch next to him. "So tell me, what were you doing out there on that bridge?" I turned and looked at him and replied, "Obviously, I was trying to kill myself."

"Do you remember any of last night?"

"A little. I know I was on the bridge and almost fell."

"Yes, and I saved your life." He looked at me as if he wanted me to say thank you. I really was grateful. I could have been dead if it wasn't for him.

"Thank you," I said in a soft voice. "Thanks a lot." He smiled and said,

"God gets the glory at the end. You're welcome though. He told me to take that route. Now I know why." He got up and went to the kitchen and came back with another glass of orange juice. "Is there any place you need to be Ailina?"

"No, what about you?"

"Not at all. It's Saturday, and I have the weekends off." What a coincidence that was. Now that I was sober and it wasn't dark, like I said before, Courtney was definitely more handsome than before. His light-brown eyes were just so gorgeous, and they had a glow in them. I couldn't stop staring at him.

"What?" he asked. "Do you need something else?" I snapped out of my little gaze and replied,

"Oh, no, sorry. I'm just very thankful that you saved my life. That's all."

"Don't mention it. But I do wanna know, why were you trying to kill yourself?" he asked. I didn't know where to start. I wanted to tell him everything, but I was gonna need the whole day. Besides, God told me to follow this man, and I believed that he was gonna be my husband. So I figured I had to play my cards right and show him that I was not just an ungrateful, stuck-up girl. A brief summary of everything was what I gave him. I told him how I lost my parents, how I was put in a mental institution, how I was held hostage by a man but never gave a name. How I wanted to get off the medication I was taking, and so on. The whole thing took at least a few minutes.

The whole time, he was looking at me in my eyes. I could tell he was about to cry himself. His eyes got watery, but he managed to hold back his tears. When I was done, there was silence for a minute. Then he broke the silence and asked, "When was the last time you had fun?"

"When my mom and dad was still alive." He got up and grabbed his car keys. He came back to me, reached for my hand, and said,

"Come with me." I took his hand, and he pulled me off the couch.

***

It was a beautiful and sunny day. His parking lot at the complex was huge. Cars were everywhere. He opened the passenger door for me and closed it when I got in. Where are we going?" I asked.

"First, I'm taking you to the mall for some shopping. Then I'm taking you to a hair salon. From there, we're gonna have some fun."

'But I don't have any money," I said.

"I didn't say you need any money. I have it all covered. Just come with me and let's have a good time."

I couldn't believe he was serious. This guy didn't even know me. All he knew was that I was some crazy girl he'd seen standing on the edge of a bridge trying to kill myself. I truly believed in my heart that this was what Sandra meant when God said follow the man who reaches out his hand for me. He did it twice. I didn't want to tell him about it yet. Only because I didn't want to mess things up or scare him off.

We arrived at the mall, and it was very busy because it was the weekend. He was making me laugh the whole time we were in the mall. His sense of humor turned me on even more. I noticed that he liked to joke and laugh. I needed that after what I'd been through. We connected so fast it was like I'd known him for years-his laughter, his smile, and his humor. Never had I met a man with so much life in him. Something about his spirit raised up and boosted my own spirit. "Come on my lady, he said. "Let's go in this dress store right here." We walked in the store, and there were dresses everywhere-pink ones, red ones, yellow ones with white polka dots, and more.

"Courtney, I love dresses!", I said.

"You like dresses, well good, because you're gonna get one." I just ran to him and gave him a nice hug. I wanted to kiss him, but I didn't know how he was going to react to that. "Pick anyone you want. We are going somewhere special later on." He had a nice smile on his face. I wondered what he did for a living. What kind of job did he have. I didn't want to ask him that either because I didn't want to seem like I was getting in his business. All the dresses were looking very pretty.

The one that stood out to me the most was the nice ruby-red pencil skirt with the silver sparkles all over it. It was one of those skirts that you didn't need a bra on with. The back side of the dress was open so that by bare back was revealed. One of the workers came over when she saw us looking at the dress. "Hello, can I help you with anything?" she asked with a friendly smile.

"Yes, ma'am. She would like to try this dress on," Courtney replied. She took the dress off the rack and showed us to the fitting room. The dress fit perfectly in the waist and top area, but it was a little too long. The sales representative advised us that I could get it altered.

"Look at the Cinderella girl," Courtney said, being funny. I smiled at him. In the meantime, while my dress was getting altered, we went to another clothing store for men. Courtney picked out an all-white suit with white slacks. When he tried it on, he looked so handsome. I pictured him wearing something like that on our wedding day.

We then stopped at a shoe store and got some nice red heels to go with my dress. When the dress was finally finished, we picked it up and headed for the exit. I had no idea what was next in line. Whatever it was, I was just gonna go with it. I wasn't gonna turn down anything he had to offer me. My plans were to play the cards right and follow him like God said.

***

We didn't put on our new wardrobe yet because he said we were gonna be too active and it would mess our clothes up. He said we were saving our clothes for the final destination. We ended up at this arcade place next. We had so much fun there. We played laser tag and arcade games. He won the first two rounds in laser tag, but I won the last round. He made me laugh the whole time. He was just so full of life. I couldn't do anything but let his spirit rub off on me. Next thing I knew, I was full of life. He won me a big stuffed animal that was a rabbit. It reminded me of the rabbit that I named Veggie in my kindergarten class.

It was time to go to our final destination. First, he took me to a hair salon that was owned by his sister. She was really sweet and offered to do my hair for free. Her name is Darlene. I asked her if I could have the wash and styles with curls. The ones I used to always get. My hair got longer and it was now just past the middle of my back. We put our new clothes on at her shop. "Thanks sis, you're the best," Courtney said as we were leaving the shop.

"You got, bro, anytime. Nice meeting you Ailina."

"Nice meeting you too. Thanks again."

We left the shop. I was looking like a supermodel in my new dress. It showed off my figure just perfectly. Courtney was just looking too handsome in his new suit. We ended up at this beautiful dining place on the other side of town. When we got out the car, the valet parker came up and gave us some assistance and parked the car for us.

The place was breathtaking when we entered. They had a nice size dance floor and live music. People were dancing, sitting at the tables, and eating dinner. There were beautiful, colorful chandeliers hanging from the ceiling. Candles were placed at the center of every table on top of red tablecloths. Waiters were walking around with trays of drinks and appetizers. Their uniforms were black pants and white dress-up shirts. The waiters had bow ties pinned to their white shirts and the waitresses had scarfs around their necks. Moments later, a waitress came over to greet us. "Good evening. Table for two?" she asked.

"Yes ma'am, table for two," Courtney answered. We followed her over to a booth by the window. We ordered our drinks first and told her we would eat later. The place was jumping with loud music and live bands. They played fast music and slow music, just like my senior prom. Courtney and I talked for a little while.

"You wanna dance?" he asked.

"Sure."

He took my hand and led me to the dance floor. We danced to the fast music. I gotta tell you, he really had some moves they started playing salsa music, and we did a little bit of salsa dancing. He taught me some moves. The man had mad skills. I didn't know he could salsa dance. I loved every minute of it. He was spinning me around and grabbing me by the waist while I wrapped my arms around is head. He spun me around and leaned me backwards. I was held in that position for a brief moment. I wanted to kiss him so bad. He ran his fingers through my hair. Then he gave me the biggest smile and lifted me back up. That was a wonderful and passionate moment.

The music was slowed down, and we slow danced. He had some moves on him I never seen on any man before. The band took a break from playing, and we went back to our table. The food was delicious. The rest of the evening, we talked and got to know each other more. "So, Ailina, I gotta tell you, you have the most beautiful hair. Have you ever cut it?"

"No, never."

"It's so silky, and I like the light-brown color."

"Thank you." I was blushing and smiling. "Can I ask you something?"

"Sure, go ahead."

"What do you do for a living?"

"I'm an operation manager for a big organization." *Wow,* I thought to myself.

"What about you?" he asked.

"I used to work at a restaurant downtown. I haven't gotten a chance to go to college yet like the rest of my friends."

"Why not?" I took a deep breath and tried to answer the question as honestly as I could.

"I just didn't want to attend college because my mental wasn't in the right place. I'm mentally unbalanced and I wouldn't have been focused on college. I'm still taking medication." That's when I realized I hadn't had an episode.

"What would you like to study if you went to college?"

"Well, I wanted to become a fashion designer. I wanted to design dresses."

"Who said you had to go to college for that? You don't know what you can do with your hands until you put them to work." I thought about that for a second. He was right. If I put my hands to work, I could design my own dresses and anything else.

"That's true," I replied. "Hey, may I use your phone for a minute. I have to call my grandparents to see where they moved to." He gave me his phone and I went to the lady's room. It felt so good to hear my grandmother's voice over the phone.

"Ailina, sweetheart, we haven't heard from you in almost a year. Where have you been?" My grandmother was so happy to hear from me. I heard it all in her voice.

"Grandma, listen. It's a long story. Something bad happened, but something good happened as well. I went by your old house the other night. Where did y'all move to?" she gave me the address, and I told her I was coming over tonight. She was so happy.

I went back to join Courtney. We talked some more, and I was giving him a little history about myself. He looked shocked when he heard I tried killing someone before. "You don't look like the type that would do such a thing," he said.

We've learned so much about each other. Courtney liked to work out and had a gym membership. And asked me to join. He asked for the bill, and we headed out of the restaurant.

We gave the valet parker the ticket, and he came back with the car. That whole day was just life changing. I believe the lord had his angels camped about me and Courtney was one of them. He saved me. I was truly grateful. The moment he would ask me to marry him, I would just jump in his arms and scream out, *YES... YES I will!*

I gave him the address to my grandparents' house. The house was bigger than the other one. We pulled up to the curb, and the night was ending. It had to be about ten O'clock pm. Man, I had a blast that night. I wish I could relive that whole day. Courtney and I had one more conversation before I got out the car. "I hope we can see each other again," Courtney said.

"Yeah, me too. I would like that very much."

"Do you have a phone number I can reach you at?"

"I don't have a phone yet, but if you give me your number, I promise I will call you." He gave me his number, and I looked him deep in his light-brown eyes and said, "Thank you again. Thank you for everything. You're truly a gentleman."

"You're very welcome." It was all God."

I liked it when he said that. I reassured me that God is alive and well. It was all him that made this thing possible for me. I unbuckled my seatbelt and gave him the biggest hug I can give him. When I was about to open the car door, he stopped me and said, "Ailina, about the medication you were taking, all you have to do is use the power of the Holy Spirit, who lives inside of you. I don't believe you need pills. You'll be totally fine." He then smiled at me.

"Okay." With that being said, I told him goodnight. I opened the car door and left.

All of the lights were on in the house, so I figured my grandparents were still up. I hesitated for a minute before ringing the doorbell. My grandfather answered. I didn't know why, but I started crying, and he held me and brought me in the house. My grandmother came down the stairs seconds later. I ran into her arms. I was so happy to see them. "We missed you so much dear. We thought something might have happened to you," my grandmother said.

"Something did happen to me. But I'm okay."

"Where did you get this pretty dress from, child?"

"I met a wonderful guy. He saved me?"

"You mean that C-Lo guy?" my grandpa asked.

"No, I got rid of him. He did horrible things to me."

"Things like what, dear?" my grandmother asked.

We sat on the living room sofa, and I told them the tale of the rocky wild side I had been on. I told them how I had been beaten and treated like a sex slave and a whore. I was embarrassed and really didn't want to talk about it. I told them how I had tried to kill myself on the bridge and how Courtney saved me. "Grandma, grandpa, please don't say I told you so. I don't wanna feel any worse than how I feel now." They agreed. "I'm sorry for the way I treated you both. I'm sorry for all the times I was being disobedient. I'll never do that to you again. I promise. I really need you guys, more than ever now." Tears came out my eyes. My grandfather put his hand on my shoulder and said,

"We're here for you, honey. You're our son's only daughter and only child. We will protect you and take care of you."

Boy was I glad to hear that. They agreed to let me stay there even after the way I mistreated them. They also agreed to buy me a new phone, and more clothes. My grandmother took me upstairs to a bedroom. It had all the rest of my things in there. She told me that they never lost hope of the fact that I will one day make my return. They had my room made up and ready to go. It had the same bed in it and the rest of my treasures- jewelry, photos of my mom and dad, and a photo of Mia.

Before I called it a night, I did what Courtney instructed me to do. I prayed. I went to bed that night thinking, *will Courtney make me his wife?* I was wondering what was gonna be next. I wondered would have happened to me if he hadn't showed up on that bridge. Only God knows. It was truly his will for me to live. All I had to do was follow the man who not once, but three times reached out his hand to me. I wanted to find out soon. I needed to find soon. I found out the very next day why God spared my life that night. It was a shocker when I found out. Something that I thought would take place months from now. And let me tell you, I didn't think I was gonna be able to handle what happened to me the next day.

Fasten your seat belts people, because this is gonna be a wild ride. Wild in a good way though. If you wanna know, you have to read the next chapter of my life.

CHAPTER 7
Things Are Looking Up

My grandparents had a garden in the backyard. My grandmother showed it to me when I woke up the next morning. Immediately, I asked if I could use it as a prayer place. She agreed. I said a prayer in the garden and believed and received what I'd prayed. It was something my mother and father taught me when I was a little girl. My grandma let me use her phone to call Courtney. He asked if he could come over and talk to me about something when he got out of church. I couldn't wait. I wanted to see him again so bad. "I would like to meet this young man name Courtney. Me and your grandmother both," said my grandpa.

"I'll cook dinner and he can come over and hang out," Grandma added.

"That sounds good. I'll ask if he's available. He said he wanted to talk to me about something anyway." I saw my grandparents were both smiling at me. I smiled back and asked, "What?"

"Ailina, when a man says he need to talk to you about something, that can be a good thing," said grandpa. "In this case, it might be a very good thing." He made me blush for a minute.

Courtney came over that evening. Right away, my grandparents liked him. He kept a smile on his face. He and my grandfather had something in common. They both liked music. Courtney's favorite artist was Zen. What a coincidence, Zen is my favorite too. He was called the Phenomenal Zen. We were sitting at the dinner table, eating a delicious meal Grandma cooked. "So, Courtney, tell me, what do you do for a living?" Grandpa asked.

"I'm an operation manager."

"Oh, that's nice. You ever had to fire someone?"

"Oh yes sir. I tell my people all the time that if you follow the rules and the policy, we won't have any problems. I never like to terminate people because we all need our jobs. Some folks took advantage of my kindness, so I had to start terminating people."

"I know what you mean my friend," my grandpa said. "Some people just have to learn I guess."

"My grandpa seemed to like him a lot. That was a good sign. After dinner, Courtney asked me to join him in his car to tell me what he wanted to say to me. First, he started asking questions, but eventually, he got to the point. It was getting close to dark, and the sun was setting.

"Ailina, it's good seeing you again. I had fun with you the other night." He smiled at me and patted my left thigh.

"Thank you. You have no idea how happy I am to see you again."

"That's good to hear. Did you have an episode by not taking your medication?"

"No, I didn't. I feel great. I have it under control now."

"That's awesome, I'm pleased to hear that."

"Listen, Courtney, I want to thank you again for the other night. You probably don't get that pretty often."

"Well, not really, but I understand good deeds doesn't go unnoticed.

"So, what is it that you want to talk to me about?" I fixed my gaze on him, waiting to hear the next words that would come from his mouth. Then he started.

"Do you believe the bible?"

"Yes," I replied.

"Do you believe that the husband is the head of the wife, and the wife is his helper?" Once again, it was something I had heard before in my early childhood. I just didn't quit understand what it meant.

"Yes, indeed I do." A smile came upon my face.

"Good," he replied. "Then I believe God is right."

"Right about what?" by this time, I was anxious. My eyes were fixed directly on him. Then he continued.

"When I went to bed last night, I asked God what the whole little bridge episode was about. I asked him why he wanted me to bring you to my home and why did I find myself washing you in my tub. I asked him what is going on. I connected with you on a level unimaginable. You wanna know what he said?" I wanted him to say it so badly. I had to know. I believed that my life was at stake for some reason. I turned all the way around to face him in the car and asked,

"What Courtney, what did he say?"

"He said, 'son, that's your wife.'" I was so excited I didn't know what to do. The smile on my face got bigger. This was all too good to be true. Someone needed to pinch me to see if I was dreaming.

"Courtney, are you asking me to marry you?"

"Please marry me, Ailina. I know we haven't known each other for a long time. I do believe in love at first sight. Yesterday was so amazing and it wasn't no coincidence we met the way we did. I truly believe in whatever the holy spirit says to me. I feel like I've known you for years. I promise I'll take care of you. I promise you'll be safe with me. I promise…

"YES…" interrupted. Him. "Yes Courtney, I'll marry you! I wanna be your helper! I wanna have your kids and live happily ever after, till death do us apart! I've only known you one day, and you stole my heart. I've been through a lot of things in my life and felt pain and misery. When I met you, that pain and misery went away."

He had a surprise look on his face. He looked as if he had a multi-million-dollar lottery ticket in his hand. Man, I never wanted to kiss him so badly as I wanted to that day. I reached over and held on to him. I gave him another one of those big hugs. For the first time in a long time, things were looking up. I couldn't wait to tell my besties Sandra and Toa. They were gonna be my two wedding parties for sure. All kinds of ideas came to my mind. The excitement of me being a wife hit me like a gust of wind. This was all too good to be true.

"Open the armrest, my dear," Courtney ordered.

"Did you want something out of it?"

"No, nothing for me, but for you." When I opened the armrest, there was a beautiful black box at the top. I grabbed the box after I gasped for air. When I opened it, I saw a beautiful diamond ring. My mouth propped opened, and I put my hand on my chest as if I was having a heart attack.

"OH MY GOD, COURTNEY, IT'S BEAUTIFUL!" I yelled. He grabbed the ring and placed it on my left index finger. "Thank you!" I don't know what to do right now. A tear fell down my face. We hugged each other so tight. He actually started to cry. I wiped his tear. "Why are you crying?" I asked.

"I've longed for a wife and I'm finally gonna have one."

I was speechless at that point. I just wished my mom and dad were here to see this. I had a vision of my dad giving me away. I pictured my mom in the front row, clapping and cheering me on. I cried again. "What's the matter?" Courtney asked.

"I just wish my mom and dad were here. That's all," I replied. He wiped my tears with his thumb very gently.

"Listen, I want you to join my church." I was willing to do anything he wanted. This was the man who God wanted me to follow. He was right. Something remarkable happened to me for being obedient and for honoring his word.

"Sure, I will. Besides, it's time that I start living for God the right way."

"Okay then. In the meantime, I want you to start thinking about who you want to be in your wedding, and I'll do the same. Let me know how many you have so I can match your number. I know some wedding planners at my church that will be willing to help plan the wedding. Don't worry about any expenses. It's already taken care of.

"That's great," I said.

"I do want to get the biblical teaching on marriage. How would you feel about marriage counseling? I wanna do right by new wife, so I want the biblical knowledge on how to work a marriage."

"That sounds find to me."

"Good, I'll fill you in with the details. Okay?" I just listened to him give orders and direct our next steps. I felt as if he was my husband already.

"Ok Courtney, I'm on board with everything." I went back inside to inform my grandparents of the news.

***

I burst in the house and ran to my grandmother who was sitting on the couch. She was reading a book with her glasses on and sipping a cup of tea. She put her book down and took her glassed off when she saw me coming. "Grandma, you won't believe what just happened to me! You won't believe it!" I fell in her arms and told her the news. "I just got engaged! He wants me to be his wife!" she put her hands over her mouth and said,

"Oh, my Lord! I'm so excited for you dear!" I lifted my hand and showed her the ring on my finger.

"It's beautiful honey." Grandpa came out of the room when he heard all the commotion.

"Is everything alright out here?" he asked.

"This child is getting married," said my grandmother.

"Oh, is that right?" he replied with a smile on his face. I showed him my ring. He walked over to the couch and pulled me up by the hand. Then he hugged me and said, "Congratulations sweetheart."

That night I went into the garden in the backyard and prayed. I gave thanks to God and thanked him for all he has done for me. I thanked him for Courtney. I thanked him for the support from my grandparents. I guess, somehow, I became infatuated with gardens. I loved the smell of the dirt and the different flowers that grew in them. My grandmother's garden wasn't all that big, but it was gonna have to do for now. I still loved it. I wanted my house to have a huge garden in the backyard. I wanted to plant all kinds of things-vegetables, flowers, and anything I could imagine.

When I was done praying in the garden, I sat down on the stairs. At first, my mind was blank. Then I started picturing myself as a wife. I pictured myself having dinner ready for my husband when he came home from work, I pictured making lunch boxes for my kids in the morning for school. I also pictured myself walking down the aisle in a beautiful white wedding dress. I pictured my hair being done in a really nice hairstyle-something other than my favorite curls.

It was amazing to me how fast things were happening. I could have been dead a long time ago. I was glad Courtney showed up on that bridge. I was glad I didn't die when I overdosed on my grandmother's pills. I had something to look forward to and was so excited about it. God's grace and mercy were upon me. I was given another chance to see the power of God.

***

So, I joined Courtney's church and met some wonderful people. The pastor was very nice. His wife, the first lady of the church, adored me. She loved my hair and my eyes. They had four awesome kids. They were very smart, and they loved their mom and dad. One of their daughters looked like me when I was younger. If only her hair was a little longer, she would be a splitting image. "What a beautiful young lady you are," Pastor Motesso said. He was a clean-cut guy who was in his early forties.

"Thank you," I replied.

"So, Courtney tells me that you both got engaged last week."

"Yes Pastor Motesso, we did." I replied.

"That's cool. He told me all about you. He also told me how you both met. That was pretty interesting. I'm very happy that Courtney can hear from God. He's a blessing to have at this congregation."

"He's definitely a blessing and also full of surprises," I said.

It was time for praise and worship, and the church was filled with people and loud music. The praise team was up on stage and little did I knew; Courtney was the leader of the praise team. He had so much energy that the whole church was just feeding off it. the songs that they were singing were just breathtaking. I joined in by dancing and singing the songs that were being sung. The live band was doing an excellent job playing the instruments. The final song was a very slow one. The keyboard guy was playing slow tones on the keyboard.

After the song was over, the pastor got on stage and said, "Come on, come on, lift those holy hands to the lord this morning. He's a mighty God!" We all lifted our hands and praised God. The soft keyboard was still playing the whole sanctuary was screaming, "Hallelujah! Thank you, Jesus!" The pastor continued, "You are so worthy today, God! Blessed be the name of the Lord this morning! Hallelujah!"

It was powerful in that place. After praise and worship, Pastor Motesso preached God's message. The message was life changing to me. The title of the message was "Fighting in the Spirit." He gave scriptures after scriptures on the Holy Spirit. It was an awesome message. The pastor was very simple and direct in his message. It was very cool, and I was calmed by it.

"See, what we don't understand is that we have the power within us given by God to overcome every obstacle that we encounter on this earth," said Pastor Motesso. "A lot of us try to fight against what we can see in the flesh but what we can see is not the battle we should be fighting against. We fight against people, and fight in our flesh. But you have to understand, that we should be fighting against principalities, powers, rulers of darkness, and spiritual wickedness in high places."

"Amen," said the whole congregation.

He continued his message. At the end of the service, I was asked if I wanted to be a part of a ministry at the church. I joined the children's ministry. Then I was asked if I wanted to be baptized in the holy spirit. I agreed and truly wanted to accept Christ as my Lord and savior.

In the middle of the week, Pastor Motesso would give baptism ceremonies. When it was my turn, I was fully submerged under the water. I came up and just started speaking in tongues. I was speaking words I wasn't familiar with. It was a totally different language. At the same time, I was crying. That was the day I died-the day I died to myself and the day Christ came alive in me.

***

I used my new phone to call my best friend, Toa. I was so happy to hear from her and hear her voice. I hadn't heard from her in almost a year. "Oh my God! Hey chica! How are you!" she said. "I've been trying to call you since forever, Are you okay?"

"I couldn't be much better, chica." I replied. I started crying. "My goodness, Toa, I missed you so much, I lot has transpired since we last talked."

"I hope they're good things."

"Some good and some bad, but I'm fine now. I have a proposition for you."

"And what's that, anything for my chica."

"How would you like to me my maid of honor at my wedding?" She screamed so loud over the phone I thought my eardrum would bust.

"I would Love to be your maid of honor! You're my favorite chica!"

"I know I am. Listen, have you heard from Sandra?"

"I talked to her yesterday. Her husband's uncle died."

"Oh no, that's not good. How sad!"

"Yea, not good. Andrew was really close to his uncle. More like a father. His uncle raised him and his sister and brother when his dad died. So he's not taking it so well."

"I know how it is losing people who raised you."

"She has a new number too. You want it?"

"Yea, hold on let me get a pen and paper." I opened my drawer and grabbed a pen and a slip of paper. She gave me Sandra's number and I put in on the nightstand. "I need to talk to her about something too."

"When is the wedding?" she asked.

"We are doing marriage counseling first. We don't have a date yet. As soon as we set one, I'll let you know.

"Ok chica."

"Toa, I really need you to come see me. Please come see me when you can." I started crying.

"Ok Ailina, I'm coming to see you. Just don't cry gurl." I wiped the tears from my face, leaned up on my bed, and pulled my hair back behind my ears so it was out of my face.

"You promise, Toa?" I really miss you, and I have to tell you everything I've been through."

"I promise chica. I miss you too, gurl." We hung up the phone and I cried again. I was happy to hear that she was coming to see me. We had known each other since kindergarten. She was the first girl I became friends with besides my childhood friend, Mia. I missed the heck out of my best friend. Immediately, I started planning some of the things that we could do and the places we could hang out at.

In the meantime, Courtney and I were doing our counseling. I was learning how to be a biblical wife. I was learning about communication, the power of oneness, being on one accord, the biblical way to love your husband and wife, and much more. As each week went by, I grew more and more excited. I was excited that I was gonna be a wife, Toa was coming to see me, and my life was changing for the better.

I called Sandra, and she was very happy to finally hear from me. It had been nearly a year.

"Oh my God, chica, I haven't heard from you in ages! How've you been!"

"I'm okay." Tears rolled down my face. "I'm so happy to hear your voice."

"Awe, Li Li, don't cry. You're making me cry now." I heard her sniffle on the other end.

"I miss y'all so much, Sandra." I started wiping the tears off my face. "Sandra, I have something to tell you. You won't believe it chica."

"Lay it on me girl."

"I'm getting married."

"Oh my God, are you serious!"

"Yes chica, he's a wonderful person and very special. I never met a man like him before. We got engaged the next day we met. I want you to be my bride's maid. Can you do that for me?"

"Of course, I can. Let me ask you a question. Why only give it one day? Isn't that too soon?"

"It's funny you ask that. Which brings me to the other thing I want to talk to you about. Remember when you died and got revived?"

"Yea."

"Well, do you remember when you told me that God appeared in the spirit realm and said for you to tell me to follow the man who reaches out his hand to me?"

"Oh yeah, I forgot all about that."

"Listen to this because this is gonna make you flip. I was on a bridge about to kill myself…"

"WHAT THE HELL DID YOU TRY TO DO THAT FOR!" she interrupted.

"Just listen. I'll explain later." I sat down at the edge of my bed and continued. "This guy pulled up and stopped when he saw me. He was very handsome and cute, gurl. He talked me out of the suicide attempt. We started talking, and he was telling me that he goes to church and everything. He asked me if I wanted kids and a husband, and a family and all that. So, I responded to him, 'yeah, I don't know what to do right now.' I said, 'what should I do?' Next thing girl, he reached his hand out and said, 'Give me your hand.'"

"Oh… my… goodness! So that's what God was talking about. I understand now. He said follow him because he knew you were gonna do that. God sent him your way to save you. Forget about my question and what

I said. You better marry him and marry him quickly gurl!" I smiled and chuckled.

"That's why I said yes when he proposed to me the next day."

I went on and on about how I almost fell off the bridge and Courtney bringing me to his house afterward. I told her about him taking me shopping, dancing, and to dinner. She was pretty amazed at that fact. She agreed to come and see me with Toa. I couldn't wait. My two friends were coming.

***

I was so happy when they arrived. It was pretty early, around six O'clock AM on a Friday. I ran up to them and hugged them both. As usual, I started crying. They looked so beautiful. Their hair was done up in our favorite curls. I took their bags and put them in my room after they greeted my grandparents. Toa said they would be staying at a hotel. My grandmother said, "Nonsense, y'all don't have to spend any money at no raggedy hotel. Y'all can stay here for the weekend." That was exactly what they did.

We caught up on some things. My grandparents were gonna give us money to go hang out. But when Courtney called me, he took that over and paid when he heard they made it in town. He came over and gave me a lot of money. "Toa, Sandra, this is my fiancé Courtney," I said.

"Nice to finally meet you ladies," he replied.

"So, I heard you saved our best friend from killing herself," said Sandra sarcastically. "You gotta excuse her sometimes."

"I'll keep that in mind," said Courtney. "Well, I see you ladies have a long day ahead of you. So, I'll get of your way and let you all be." Toa held up her pointy finger and said,

"Not so fast there lover boy, hold up a second. Just why did you decided to be so nice to our bestie anyway?" He turned around looked me. Then he smiled and replied,

"Because God told me too." With that, he winked and then left.

We had some fun that weekend. It was more than fun. It was a blast. We went to our favorite mall. Almost every guy who passed our way was trying to talk to us. At the food court area, some guy was hitting on me in line getting some food. He wasn't attractive at all. Number 1, I had a fiancé,

76

number 2, he tried too hard, and number 3, he couldn't dress. No matter how many times I was trying to tell him I was already involved with someone, he would not listen-not until Sandra stepped in and let him have it. "Listen, jerk. How many times does she have to tell you that she already has a fiancé?" he rubbed the hairs on his chin while smiling. Then he used the oldest punch line in the book, so old that the dinosaurs were saying it.

"Whatcho man got to do with me?"

That was the last straw for Sandra. She flagged down one of the mall cops who was passing by while saying,

"Security, can you come over here please!" The mall cop came over and asked,

"Is everything ok over here?"

"This guy is harassing my friend. Can you get him away from here, please?" He snatched the guy up and he was escorted out of the mall.

We finally ate our food in peace, laughing and joking around with each other. They both told me that they would be moving back when they were done with college. I was happy to hear that. I cherished every moment with my girls, sitting at our table, eating our lunch and enjoying ourselves. We talked about my wedding and how things would go. We set up dates for the rehearsal. They agreed to come back in a few months to get the ball rolling.

"Are you ready to be a wife, Li Li?" Toa asked.

"Of course, the marriage counseling we are going through is helping me a lot. My favorite part is the biblical role of a wife."

"I love being a biblical wife," Sandra said. "My husband calls me his virtuous woman all the time." She took a sip of her soda.

"I'll be a wife soon," said Toa.

"And when that time comes, I want to be the maid of honor," I said.

"You know you will."

After we ate, we shopped for outfits and new pairs of shoes. We took all day shopping. When we were done, we left the mall and sucked up the nice Tampa Bay weather on the sandy beaches. It was hot as ever, and we had on our bathing suits. The waves from the blue waters were rushing up on the sand. People were running toward them and flopping into the ocean. I called Courtney to come and pick up our bags and take them home. As usual, guys were looking at us with their tongues hanging out like dogs. We laid out blankets on the sand that Courtney brought to us and sat down.

"Oh man, I missed this wonderful Florida weather, Toa said.

"So do I," Sandra replied.

Eventually we hopped into the water and cooled off. We stayed at the beach until the sun went down. it was lovey that day. My grandmother had some bakery snacks ready for us. The night was falling, and it was getting darker outside. It was still humid out. I raised my window up so we can feel some breeze. It was barely breeze because of the humidity. We took our showers and hung out in my room for the rest of the night. Sandra was still taking her shower, and so, Toa and I talked while sitting on my bed.

"Your hair is longer than the last time I've seen you. It's so beautiful, and it has a rich color to it," she said.

"Thanks. I have my mother's hair texture." After I said that, I held my head down. she sensed the fact that I was getting emotional. She scooted closer to me.

"You miss her huh?" she asked. A tear came down my face.

"Yes. I miss both of them. I just wish I could snap my fingers and bring them back." I cried harder. She held me, and I just cried in her arms.

"Listen chica. You have two wonderful friends who loves you, two grandparents who will do anything for you, and a fiancé who adores you. You're not alone my sister. We all love you." I nodded my head up and down. she brushed my hair to the back of my ear with her hand and said, "you're my best friend Li Li. We've been best friends since kindergarten. You know you can always talk to me. Is there something you want to talk about?" I took a deep breath.

"I was in an abusive relationship."

"WHAT!" she yelled.

"Shhhh! I think my grandparents are sleeping."

"What kind of punk ass son of a bitch put his hands on my chica!"

"He's long gone now. He took my phone from me, and I wasn't allowed to talk to anyone. That's why you and Sandra haven't heard from me, in almost a year." I saw in her eyes that she wasn't very happy.

"And all this time, I thought you just forgot about us," she said.

"Of course not. I was forced to have sex with different men for money. I would do the work, and he will collect the money.

"So, he was pimping you!" She grew angrier.

"Yeah, but different men were coming to the house I wasn't allowed to go anywhere."

"I can't believe what I'm hearing! I don't understand why some guy would want to treat a beautiful young woman like that! I'm sorry you had to go through that Li."

"I blame myself. My grandparents were trying to warn me about things like that. I totally blew them off. That's why I was trying to kill myself that night. If it wasn't for Courtney, I was gonna be dead."

"You wanna know something," she asked.

"Sure, what's that?"

"When I called you one day, a man answered your phone. He told me to never call again or he will kill me."

"Wow, that had to be him." Sandra walked in. she flopped down on the bed.

For the rest of the night, we talked. I told them the rest of the story of how I was treated by C-Lo and how Courtney saved me. We laid in my bed under the covers. We didn't go to sleep until about two in the morning. Toa was telling me how much she missed Mia. She actually cried. So did I. for the rest of the weekend, we just had so much fun. I didn't get emotional and cry when it was time for them to leave. I knew they would be back anyway.

***

They came back months later to meet with the wedding planners and go over some things for my wedding. The theme of the wedding was chosen to be angels. I chose that because I believed that angels had been protecting me all my life. I knew I had me some angels. Just thinking about it, what could have happened to me if I never went straight home when Sandra was viciously attacked coming from the movies? That could have been me. Let's not forget about all the failed suicide attempts. The colors for my wedding were pink and white.

We finished our marriage counseling and got the marriage license soon after. The date was set, and time was ticking. When Toa and Sandra came back, we shopped for bridesmaid dresses and my wedding dress. The dresses were asked to be pink with white dress shoes. I was getting happier and happier. We had fun shopping for the dress. my grandmother went with us. The wedding day was a month away.

I tried to call Courtney, but he didn't answer his phone. That wasn't like him because he always answers his phone when I called. I waited a little while and tried to call him again. Still there was no answer. Immediately, I began to worry. For the rest of the day, I didn't hear from him. I tried to call, and there was no answer. I was so worried I didn't know what to do. I called people at the church, and they said they hadn't heard from him either. "I'm sure he'll call you back, dear. He is about to get married. Maybe he's taking some time to himself to think," my grandmother said while I was laying on her lap crying.

"I miss him grandma, what if something happened to him?"

"Non sense child. Just give him a while. He'll call you."

"I love him grandma! I love him!" I was thing that maybe he wanted to call the wedding off and was too ashamed to tell me.

People at the church were saying they hadn't heard from him in a long time. Even Pastor Motesso hadn't heard from him. That was unusual. Because he always talked to pastor Motesso. I got even more scared. I blew his phone up every day, trying to contact him. It had been over a week and still no luck. I stayed in my room, crying on my bed. My legs were shaking, and I thought he really had left me. When I kept trying to call, there was no ring. It went straight to voicemail. I left messages after messages. Where was he? Was he a victim of foul play? Where in the heck was my soon-to-be husband? I went into the garden to pray that he will make his return.

CHAPTER 8
Another Tragedy

I grew more and more frustrated. Two weeks passed, and I still hadn't heard from Courtney. I assumed the worst. Every time my phone ring, I thought it was Courtney. I was disappointed every time. My heart was broken. So, I just stopped calling. My grandparents were trying to cheer me up. Nothing they did worked. The thought came through my mind that maybe this isn't the guy for me.

One day, I went for a walk after I got through from praying in my grandparents' garden. I prayed that Courtney would return and gave thanks to the Father. I walked to a local park. It was hot that day. Kids were playing on the slides and swinging on the swings, and people were walking their dogs around the walk pathways. I sat down on the bench, looking like and old lady waiting for her long-lost love to return. My head was held down, and my hands were folded together on my lap. My phone rang, and it was my grandmother. She was asking me if I'm okay. I said yes. Really, I wasn't. I continued walking along the pathway. Tears were falling. I couldn't believe Courtney had left me. I wondered if he had left me for another female. The thought of that just made me cry even more. I missed him so much. This couldn't be right. Why would God put this man in my life, tell me to follow him, and then take him from me?" I wiped the tears from my face.

I came across a pond with ducks swimming in it. A couple and their daughter were feeding them. I stopped and watched. The little girl ran towards me and gave me a piece of bread to throw at the ducks. Very softly she said, "Here, take one, they don't bite. I took the bread and threw it to the ducks. By me throwing the bread was a sign to me not to be scared. She smiled at me and ran back to her parents.

I walked some more down the path. I sat down on benches every so often to rest a little while. I thought some more on the whole situation. He had to be okay. He just had to be. The wedding was getting near. He had to come back to me. I finally walked back home.

Toa called me that evening to check on me. "Hey chica, did he call you back yet?" she asked.

"No, I'm so hurt right now, Toa. I don't know what to do."

"Something must have happened. Not to him. It might be family related. Maybe he doesn't want you involved,"

"Toa, you can be right. But why wouldn't he want me involved? I'm his fiancé."

"I don't know. I hope you're not giving up on this. I almost gave up on college."

"Why?"

"All these papers and assignments that I be having to do. It's so overwhelming I can just pull my hair out gurl."

It had been nearly three weeks since I heard from Courtney. I was still making preparations for the wedding. I've been meeting with my wedding coordinator, and my two wedding parties Toa and Sandra. They were making the preparations to come down for the special event. I wondered, *what if Courtney doesn't make his return before the wedding?*

One morning, I came back in the house from praying in the garden. My phone rang. I didn't bother looking at the caller ID because I thought it would be either my wedding coordinator, Sandra or somebody. Very softly I said, "Hello." Courtney's voice was on the other side telling me to come outside. I put my shoes on quickly as I could and ran out the door. I ran to his car and got in. As soon as I entered, I just snapped like I never snapped before. "What the hell is wrong with you Courtney!" He was just staring into space with a blank look on his face. He looked as if he had been crying. I continued. "I haven't heard from you in weeks! I was worried sick about you!" I started crying myself.

He didn't bother to look at me. The look on his face was just blank, as if he had lost something very valuable. I kept yelling. Finally, he slowly turned his head to look at me. He placed his hand on mine very gently. Then he spoke. "You know, I remember one time my mother told me not to do something, and I did it anyway. She told me not to be jumping off garages. My friends and I would jump off garages and onto bed mattresses. We got caught. My mom took a belt and tore my behind up with it." He giggled a little bit. "She told me something very vital when she was done. I was in my room, sitting on my bed. She came in and sat next to me. She said," 'son, I didn't punish you because you were jumping on of the garage. It was mainly because you were disobedient. It's gonna come a time when you will have to learn to be obedient. I'm not gonna be on this earth forever. Someone will always be in charge of you and you have to learn how to respect your authority figures.'"

I didn't know what the point of him telling me that story was at that moment. I got back to the matter at hand. "Why haven't I heard from you Courtney? Don't you know I cried night and day for you? *Damn you!* I thought I lost you!"

"Sorry Ailina. I just buried my mother out of town." My heart sank. I felt so bad for yelling at him. I knew how it was to lose a mother. I could just imagine the pain he was going through.

"Oh my God Courtney, I'm so sorry! I didn't know." I leaned over and held him as he cried in my arms. I cried with him. I kept repeating, "I'm sorry, I'm so sorry. God told me to follow you, and I thought I lost you."

"It's okay baby. You didn't know."

"Why didn't you tell me? I could have come with you and been of a good support."

"You lost your parents already, not to mention Mia and almost losing your friend Sandra. I didn't want another count on your list. I didn't call you because I knew you would want to come, and I didn't know how to say no to you. I'll never leave you baby. I'm sorry for putting that worry and stress on you. Let's go for a ride, okay?"

"Yeah, sure."

***

We drove off and ended up going to the beach, the same one Toa and Sandra and I went to when they were here visiting me. We walked and talked while holding hands. I could vouch for the fact that he didn't want me to come because I experienced enough deaths in life already. It was so sweet of him to think about me like that. He was right. I don't really do so well with funerals. Look at how I acted at my parents' funeral. We walked on the deck surrounded by the blue water. "How did she die?" I asked.

She had been battling a sickness for years. It finally caught up with her and finished her off."

"Courtney, you're so amazing to me," I said.

"What's so amazing about me?"

"For me personally, the way you saved my life that night, the way you took me to your house and took care of me, taking me shopping and dancing. You didn't even know me. You acted like I was already your wife. It's like you're already my husband. When we get married, I want to give you all I have. I want to give you my body, my love, and I want you to rule over me like God said for you to do. When you disappeared, I thought you left me for another woman. All kinds of thoughts were going through my mind. I don't know what I would do without you. I was so scared, Courtney." He turned to face me then he replied,

"Baby, I'll never leave you. You're my best friend and my soon to be wife. God gave me this heart. It's all him." He took both of my hands. "I like hanging out with you. I like making you laugh. You're so beautiful. You have hair like a royal princess. You're eyes just light up my world when I look into them. Just know, I'll never leave you. You wanna know why?" I looked him in the eyes and asked,

"Why?"

"Because I love you. I Love everything about you. I love you unconditionally as Christ loves the church. My love for you will never go away because I love you like God loves you. His love never fails or goes away." Tears came down my face-tears of joy.

"I love you too Courtney." That was the moment I knew one hundred percent he's for me.

He hugged me and planted his lips on my forehead. That was the first time a man told me he loved me, besides my dad and my grandfather. Not even C-Lo ever told me he loved me. That was because it was obvious that he didn't. I was just a sex tool to him. That day on the deck with Courtney was so magical to me. Courtney said he loved me. When he told me that, chills went down my spine. I couldn't wait until we got married. I wanted to show him how much I really loved him.

"Let's go back to my place," he said.

We left the beach and went back to his apartment. He made us some salads with homemade lemonade drinks. The death of his mother actually brought the two of us closer. It sealed the deal, if that's how you wanna put it. we sat at his table and talked some more. "Ailina, what did you mean when you said, 'God said for you to follow me?'" he asked. I took a sip of my lemonade and answered the question.

"Remember my friend Sandra?"

"Yeah, the one who was viciously attacked and almost died?"

"Yes, she told me something that eventually made sense." He took a forkful of his salad.

"What did she tell you?" he asked.

"Well, it's like this. She died and got revived. Then she told me God appeared to her in the spirit realm." I held my head down and took a deep breath before I continued. "She told me that God told her to tell me to follow the man who reaches out his hand for me." His eyes got big.

"Wow," he said. That's powerful. It all makes sense now."

"What makes sense?" I asked.

"I wasn't gonna take that route home. God told me to take the bridge. The reason why he made me take that bridge was for me to save you and take your hand so you can follow me."

"Well, I'm glad you took that route," he smiled at me.

"I have something to tell you", he said.

"What's that?"

"I got a promotion at my job!"

"Really! Congratulations! What did you get promoted to?"

"I got promoted to RVP, Region Vice President."

"Oh wow, Courtney! That's amazing!" I got up and gave him a hug.

"I will be over all of the accounts in my region. You wanna hear some more news?"

"Yes. Yes, I do!"

"I'm moving out of this apartment, and I already found a house for us." I got so excited. I was happier than a kid at their favorite amusement park. I hugged him tight as I could.

The wedding day was on day away. Toa and Sandra made it in the day before. Sandra told us that she was having a baby. She said she wanted to tell us face-to-face to see the expression on our faces. We were so happy for her. We went over the rehearsal at the church. I was told not to see the groom before the wedding day. That whole day was, by far, the busiest day ever. Wedding rehearsals, getting my dress altered, making sure my coordinator was on point, etc. I missed Courtney the entire day. My wedding party and I all went out for dinner. It was lot of us. My grandmother even came.

***

It was finally less than seven hours away from the wedding. I went to the hair salon of Courtney's sister and let her do my hair. She hooked me up really good. She washed my hair and put it in the most beautiful style I had ever seen. The makeup artist put a little bit of eyeliner around my eyes and a little mascara. My face was glittery. Everyone was telling me how beautiful I looked. We went to the church and got dressed there. It was decorated so nice. Pink-and-white bow ties on the edge of the pews with pink and white ribbons hanging from the ceiling.

It was time for me to come out and meet my husband at the altar. Everyone stood up when they heard our wedding song. I grabbed my grandfather by the arm as he led me to the altar and gave me away. I cried for sure. I saw my husband standing there at the altar, waiting for me. He looked so handsome in his all-white-tux and white slacks. I wanted to just run to him. His hair was freshly cut but still short and curly.

I finally reached him, and he took my hand. The praise team sang a few songs and slowed it down with a Christian wedding song. We exchanged vows, and the pastor finally said the words I'd been dying to hear ever since I met Courtney. "By the power invested in me, I know pronounce you husband, and wife. Courtney, you may kiss your bride!" Courtney lifted the veil over my face and planted his lips on mine. It was the most amazing kiss ever. It was even more amazing than when I tongue-kissed Billy Rogers.

The ceremony was lovey. The reception was held at Pastor Motesso's home. His backyard was huge as ever, and so was his house. Everything was just perfect. Toa and Sandra couldn't stay long. They had to leave for their flight. My husband and I shared a dance on the dance floor. We slow danced for a long time. He whispered in my ear, "Baby, guess what." I lifted my head to look at him.

"What, honey?" It felt good calling him that.

"The congregation all pitched in, and they are sending us away for the weekend."

"That's so sweet. Where are they sending us to?"

"On a cruise."

"Wow, I can't wait!"

"I have a surprise for you when we get back." All these surprises were almost overwhelming.

"What is it? Can I know now?"

"Nope, this one will have to wait. I wanna see the expression on your face for this.

We left and went on our cruise. Everyone on board had their own rooms. My husband and I had ours as well. The first night was just awesome. The events there were pretty fun. We tried to participate in all of them. They had events for married couples, individuals, and also children. The night was ending, and we just came back to our room after and event calling knowing your spouse. "Wow Ailina, you did pretty good tonight. I can't believe you beat me," my husband said.

"I guess I know you pretty well, huh?" he picked me up, and I wrapped my legs around him. He held me up against the wall. Then he said,

"You might have won the game, but you're not gonna win this game we're about to play." We shared a long passionate kiss. Next thing I knew, we ended up on the king size bed. He was on top of me while I was unbuttoning his shirt. He then zipped down my black leather shirt and my bra was showing. He began to kiss me again. I grabbed his face and wrapped my lets tighter around his waist. He took his hand and grabbed my right breast. I wanted him to touch me. I wanted him to touch all over and anywhere he wanted. That's exactly what he did. I couldn't help myself. I took control and got on top of him. Seconds later, I unsnapped my bra so that my breasts could be exposed to him. He took his hands and grabbed both of them, putting them in his mouth.

We made love for hours and hours. For the first time, I didn't feel like a whore. I didn't feel like I was doing something wrong. This was my husband-the man God said to follow. I would follow him as he followed Christ. It was obvious to me that he had done this before. The way he handled me was just like a man fixing his car. He knew what he was doing. He knew what parts go where how fast or slow to go, if you know what I mean.

The second night was fascinating as well. We made love like there was no tomorrow. At the end of the trip, we made it back to our home. I couldn't believe the house that my husband purchased for us. It was beautiful, with a two-car garage, three bedrooms, and stainless-steel appliances. He blindfolded me and took me outside to show me the real surprise. When he took off the blindfold, my world lit up like a Christmas tree. Before me was a gigantic, beautiful garden. In it were flowers, veggies, plants, and more flowers. "Oh my God Courtney, it's so beautiful!" I turned and planted a kiss directly on his lips. "Thank you honey, I love you so much!"

"I love you too baby."

Of course, I used my garden as a prayer place. It became my place to dwell with the lord and give thanks to him. I did that every morning. I truly believe that all this was for me-Courtney showing up, a beautiful home surrounded by people who care for you, and on top of that, still living life on God's green earth. I was proud of myself and my husband. He had worked so hard for his promotion and had gotten a house. I loved him for it. I couldn't be any more proud-proud to be called Ailina C. Maynord.

CHAPTER 9
The Biblical Wife

My new husband and I got settled in hour new place. He let me decorate the whole house. My favorite place was my prayer garden. I used it every time I felt sad, angry, frustrated, bitter, and all the other negative words you can think of. Getting used to the married life was somewhat hard and somewhat easy. I had to make sure I knew what my husband likes as far as food and what he didn't like. He didn't like baked chicken. He always preferred it to be fried, grilled, or even boiled. His favorite vegetables were carrots, green beans, cabbage, greens, potatoes, and broccoli. After six months into our marriage, I was starting to get the hang of being a biblical wife.

Courtney was also trying to get used to me as well. I was more complicated. But not on purpose. On or date nights, I would say I wanted to go one place and then change my mind at the last minute and say another place. This irritated him because he hated last minute split decisions. He was the type of person to plan out his day and go according to what was planned. Me, on the other hand, was the opposite. My day could go by without planning anything. We got used to each other though. At least for the most part. People change over time. We just had to keep up with each other. We would argue once in a while. That was normal for married couples. We disagreed on lots of things, but together, we worked them out. The Word of God had the final authority.

Courtney was also getting used to his new position. It was hard work for him-new wife and new sets of rules at his job. I was there for him anytime he needed me. One day, he came home from work so tired and overwhelmed with all the reports he had to write for his bosses about what was going on at his accounts. He had to fire one of his account managers because it was proven that he was having sexual relationships with some of the female employees. So, my husband had to write up a report about that as well. He just flopped down on the couch and laid down. I had just come inside from planting new plants in my prayer garden. "Hey honey," I said, as I greeted him with a warm hug and kiss.

"Oh, hey baby, how are you?" he sat up so he could greet me properly. I sat on his lap and rubbed his chest.

"I'm fine. You want something to eat?"

"Yeah, sure. Nothing too heavy though." I went into the kitchen and fixed him a shrimp pasta dish with a salad. When I came back in the living room he had nodded off. He wasn't in a deep sleep, just a little catnap. I tapped him on his arm and whispered,

"Honey… honey the food is ready." He rosed up and walked into the dining room. I joined him at the dining table. "Courtney, I have an idea."

"Oh yea, what's that?"

"I want to be a clothes designer, specifically dresses." He looked up at me and rubbed his chin.

"What kind of dresses?"

"I'm not sure, maybe wedding dresses, prom dresses, whatever I can get my hands on." I could tell the idea was exciting to him. I knew when he was surprised or in a deep thought because he would squint his eyes and stare into space. "I take it as you like the idea?"

"Yeah. It's funny you said that because I know a lady at my headquarter building who designs dresses for various stores. She actually just opened up her own clothing store a month ago. She comes into my office and shows me pictures of some of the dresses she designed. I can talk to her for you."

"Really!" I smiled out of excitement.

"Yea, I'm good friends with her. She trains people on how to make dresses and hires them. Maybe she can teach you, and you can start up your own business."

He talked to her the next day. She agreed to teach me everything I needed to know. She showed me the different equipment and what they were used for. Her name was Francis. She was very kind. Francis was no more than about forty to forty-five years of age. She was Caucasian with short blond hair. She offered to teach me free of charge because she was good friends with my husband. I met up with her at her home. We got started, and she taught me all the things I needed to know.

After one of the sessions, I drove home and had to pull over. I pulled over because my stomach got a little woozy. That same night, I got up out of the bed and ran to the bathroom. I threw up in the toilet. My husband heard the commotion and ran into the bathroom. "What's wrong baby?" he asked.

"I don't know, I've been feeling like this all day."

"Maybe it's just a twenty-four- hour virus."

I went back to bed, and the next morning I was sick again. It was about six O'clock in the morning. Courtney was in the shower, getting ready for work. I ran into the bathroom and threw up again. He slid the shower door open and yelled, "Baby, are you okay?" I couldn't respond at all. I just shook my head no. He agreed to stay home and take me. He took me to see the doctor.

"How long have you been throwing up, Mrs. Maynord?" Dr. Stilton asked.

"About twenty-four hours." I replied.

"I was guessing it was just a twenty-four- hour virus," said Courtney.

"When did you last have your menstrual cycle, Mrs. Maynord?"

"I don't remember."

"Well, I think I know what the problem is." He did an ultrasound on me and then began to explain what was on the monitor. "You see that little outline area here? That's a head. You see that flicker? That's a heartbeat. Looks like you're pregnant my dear."

I looked at Courtney, and he looked at me. We both smiled at each other. He came over and hugged me. "How far along Doc?" I asked.

"I'd say you are a little more than a month into your pregnancy. Congratulations!"

We were so happy. I started to think about something. Out of all those sexual activities with those other guys, I didn't get pregnant. But when I got sexually active with my husband, I got pregnant. This was all God for sure. It wasn't his will for me to get pregnant by those other guys. I wondered what I was having. If it was a girl, I wanted to name her after my mother in her honor, Jan.

***

I gave birth to a beautiful healthy baby girl. My husband was by my side the whole time, and so were my grandparents. When she came out, I heard her sweet, innocent cry. I named her Jan. Sandra had her baby months before I had Jan. She had a boy and named him Andrew Jr.

A year later, my classes and training with Francis were complete. I learned all I needed to know to design dresses and other clothes. My husband brought me the materials and equipment I needed. I began to make clothes and dresses for several people, even people at the church.

It wasn't long until God gave me the idea to start a business. Everything fell into place. For starters, I rented a small space downtown. I used that space to work out of, as far as making the dresses and showing other people how to make them. The business started to progress, grossing a lot of money. I named my shop Ailina's dress design. It was gaining so much business I had to open up more stores. I worked with other clothes designers to make the clothes and dresses.

I got compliments on how well the dresses were designed. The customers would email me on what a good job my workers and I were doing. My husband was so proud of me. My boutique stores were doing so well it was almost scary. The goodness of God was hovering over me. I made sure he received every tenth from my income for tithes and offering. I had to give back to God. My husband and I became a blessing to the kingdom.

Because my business grew into an empire, I had to work out and operate out of my headquarter building. My office was at the very top level. I made trips on and off at the eleven different locations throughout the state of Florida. My logo was a small image shaped as a garden with the letter *A* at the top. My clothes and shoes were top of the line. My office phone would blow up with people asking me when I would be making new dresses and outfits.

So, I had my business going, and my husband was RVP of his company. I was asked to be in charge over the children's ministry at the church. I agreed. I wanted to be spiritually employed as well as self-employed. Courtney was still in charge of the praise team. My daughter, who was now three, loved playing with the other kids. She looked so much like her dad it wasn't even funny. Her long light-brown-hair swung around while she ran and played around the day care room.

Toa and Sandra finally moved back to Florida after they were done with college. I had my two friends with me again. Toa broke the news to us that she was finally getting married to a guy she met in college. I was the maid of honor. The three of us hung together all the time. They also joined local churches.

I made it home from my office one evening and heard Courtney talking to his boss on the phone. He was yelling. I walked into the kitchen where he was and sat next to him by the counter. He seemed very upset. "I can't believe this Floyd! How could he do that?" he put his hand on his forehead, as if he received some terrible news. "I'll find out if he's doing that for sure. I'm gonna launch a full investigation immediately." Then he hung up the phone.

"Is there something wrong honey?" I asked.

"Oh yeah! Very wrong."

"What is it?"

"One of the account managers in my region is suspected of embezzling money from the company."

"What are you gonna do?" He got up and went into the refrigerator and grabbed a bottle of water.

"My boss wants me to go with him out of state to visit the account."

"Are you leaving me?"

"I'll try to be back as quick as possible."

"How long are you gonna be gone for, honey?" I almost yelled.

"No longer than a week."

"Can you tell him that you can't do it? I don't wanna be away from you for a week!" What am I gonna do without you?"

"I don't know Ailina. I'm the Vice President of the region, and it requires me to travel."

"Can I come? Jan and I?"

"No, Floyd made it very clear that I have to be flexible. And besides, you have your business to look after." That angered me so bad. I stormed off and went upstairs to the bed room. He came after me. I flopped down on the bed and held my head down. "Ailina, I can't do this with you right now. You're not making it any better by acting like that." Jan came walking into the room, playing with her toys. "Hi sweetheart," Courtney said. She ran to him, and he picked her up.

"Hi daddy!"

"How's daddy's little girl?" I almost got emotional. I had a flashback when my mother and father said that to me.

"Hungry," she said.

"You want mommy to fix you something to eat?"

"Yeah!" I got up off the bed and took her from Courtney.

"Come on tuts," I said. She reached out her arms to me.

I went downstairs and made her favorite buttered fried, ham and cheese sandwich. She liked for the cheese to be melted really good. When she was done, it was time for her nap. I rocked her back and forth on the couch until she fell asleep. Then I took her back upstairs and laid her in her bed. Courtney was in the office room, sitting in front of the computer. I went in and made up for the little fight we had. He looked up at me when he saw me enter the room. "Is she sleep?" he asked.

"Yes, sound asleep." I walked around the desk to where he was at. "Baby, listen. I'm sorry. I didn't mean to be so selfish. I just don't like it when you're gone for a long time. You understand that right?" he grabbed my arm, spun me around and sat me on his lap.

"Of course baby, I understand. This will all be over soon. Okay?"

"Okay honey." I placed my lips on his and kissed him softly. "So when are you leaving?"

"In two days."

"What's gonna happen if the manager is indeed stealing from you guys?"

"I'm gonna have no choice but to fire him. Imma fire him quickly. He doesn't know that we're on to him yet. This is a surprise visit to the account."

"Okay, go get him, baby!"

***

I dropped my husband off at the airport two days later. I had plans to go with some church members to dinner. My grandparents agreed to watch Jan. Sandra and Toa came with me. I introduced them to my church family members. They didn't get to officially meet at the wedding. At the end of our dinner date, Toa and Sandra came back to my house after I picked up my baby. "Look at how much progress we've made over the years!" Toa said. We were sitting in my living room, watching a movie. Sandra had her son with her since her husband worked the night shift.

"I know. It's the goodness of God that we made it this far," I replied.

"Hey Li Li, you think you can do me a favor?" Toa asked.

"Sure. What's up chica?"

"Okay, check this out. I know someone who has a daughter who will love it if you design a prom dress for her. I told her I will talk to you. I didn't guarantee anything. I just said I will ask you. Maybe give her a little discount under the table?" That was the first time I was asked to do such a thing. I thought about it for a minute, and I came to my decision.

"Good thing you caught me three months in advance.", I said. I went into my purse and took out one of my business cards and handed it to Toa. "Give her my card. Tell her I'll do it for her."

"Okay chica. She's gonna be highly appreciative of this." Jan and Jr. were on the floor, playing with toys and eating snacks. Those two liked playing with each other.

"Don't get anything on my floor little ones," I said. "Sandra, Jr. looks so much like his dad!"

"I get that a lot. He looks nothing like me."

"He has your nose though," Toa said. We hung out until ten PM. The kids passed out on the floor.

I woke up the next morning and went into by prayer garden to pray. I gave my thanks to the Father and prayed in the spirit to build up my inner man. The soil looked a little dry, so I watered my whole garden. I went back into the house to see if my daughter was up. She was still asleep. I took a shower and made breakfast for the two of us. I fed her when she woke up. After that, I got her washed up. For that day, we would be at the park. "You're ready tuts?" I asked, while I as putting her in her car seat. She smiled at me and nodded her head up and down. it was something I used to do when my parents asked me something that I was happy about.

My baby was so excited, running around barefooted in the sand, chasing after the other kids, and drinking refreshments. I decided to go to my headquarter office and check up on things. Also, I wanted to see if I had any important calls. I sat Jan down on my couch in my office while I looked over some paperwork. Nothing really important was there. Then I got a phone call on my cell phone. "Hey queen! How's my virtuous woman!" It was my husband.

"Hey honey! I'm great. How are things going so far with you?"

"Man, you will never believe it. My boss is so happy with me right now it's pathetic! I'll tell you all about it when I get back. Looks like I'll be back earlier than I thought. It didn't take long for me to do my investigation."

"That's good baby! I can't wait to see you! I'm just leaving my office."

"Okay, I can't wait to see you either."

I went back home after making a few runs. I stopped to purchase more plant seeds for my garden. Thank goodness, I decided to water my garden that morning. The sun was beaming hard. Jan was playing with her toys on the patio area while I was planting the seeds. When I got done, I took Jan and went back into the house. I had grown hungry after working in my garden. So I whipped up some sandwiches for my daughter and me.

When I went back to my office the next day, I got a message from the lady who wanted me to design a prom dress for her daughter. The lady's name was Sue. I called her back and agreed to meet at my office the same day. She looked like she was too young to have a teenage daughter. She was very attractive. She had pretty long black hair. She had the figure of a very young lady. She came in and sat down on my couch. "It's very nice to meet you... Sue, isn't it?", I said.

"Yes, good to meet you as well, Ailina I heard so much about you." I gave her a real nice personal discount because she was so kind and polite. I began to work on the dress. her daughter's favorite color was yellow. I got her waist size and height as well. I worked on it downstairs in the basement where my equipment was at. I took my time with it.

It was almost a week since Courtney had been gone. He finally called to inform me that his flight will be landing in about six hours due to a delay. I got another phone call from Sandra I couldn't believe the news she told me. "Hey, chica, you will never guess who's back in town!" she said.

"And who is that?" I asked.

"Billy Rodgers!"

"Oh my God, are you kidding me right now!" You can't be serious!" I didn't know whether to be happy or what. I did have a crush on him in high school. "I wonder what made him come back here," I said.

"He said that his family had to come back to take care of his sick grandmother. He asked for your number. I told him you were married now. He didn't take that too well."

"What did he say?"

"He said he never should have left the state. So, what do you think, should I give him your number?" I didn't know what to think either. I was speechless for a minute. Then I said,

"Give me his number. I'll call him soon."

"He can't wait to hear from you."

"I'm sure he can't." The hours passed, and I packed up Jan in the car and left to pick up my husband.

***

I met up with Courtney at the baggage claim area. He had on a nice business suit, and his hair looked curlier than before. "Hey, baby!" he said. After greeting me with a kiss. Then he greeted Jan. At home I helped unpack, and he told me all about what happened while I was helping him undress in the bedroom. "So, when we got there, he was so surprised. He tried to play it off like everything was fine. I told him that I would need an accounting of where the money was going. That didn't turn out so well. So what I did was, I went to the bank and got the statements from them. What I found out was that there was money being transferred into another account. I tracked the account right back to his personal account."

"Wow," I said. "So, what did you do next?"

"I fired him on the spot. I told him to pack up his things and leave my account."

"Dang, you're so tuff honey! How did he take that?"

"He tried to fight me in front of the employees. He was yelling and screaming at me and my boss. It was crazy! You should have been there!"

"Wow! Interesting. So, what's gonna happen to the account?"

"For the time being, we have the training-develop-coordinator, AKA Chief of Staff person taking over until I hire another training coordinator. So basically, the training coordinator is the new account manager. One month from now, I will have to go back to the account and interview applicants for the position. I gotta post the position for a month, ordered by Floyd, the boss."

"Okay, I'm proud of you, baby!" I gave him a long passionate kiss on the lips. "I'm designing a prom dress for the daughter of a lady Toa knows."

"Oh cool. Do you have some ideas?"

"Yea. It's gonna take me a little while. Courtney, I have something to tell you." I took a deep breath and walked toward him.

"What's that baby?" He kicked of his shoes and laid flat at the head of the bed.

"Someone I used to go to high school with is back in town, and I wanted to say I."

"Oh, okay. Well, say hi to her then."

"The thing is that it's a guy." He sat up on the bed and cleared his throat. Then he said,

"Well, I don't mind you saying hi."

"You don't?"

"No, not at all. You're a woman of God now. I have faith in you. I'm not gonna stop you from having friends." I crawled up on the bed and slowly crawled up towards him. My hair was almost touching the bed. Then I kissed him and slipped him the tongue. It was like how I kissed Billy Rogers.

We heard Jan walk in the room with her favorite doll in her hand. She had the biggest smile on her face. She was smiling as if she as was saying, *awwww, that's so sweet.*

I got up off the bed, and she came running to me. I picked her up and jokingly said,

"Are you spying on us, little one?" I tickled her on her stomach. She laughed hard. I kissed her on the cheek. "We have to go the store.", I said.

"We can go tomorrow. I'm tired."

"For the rest of the day, we just chilled out and relaxed. I cooked dinner and watched the late news in the living room with my family. They were still talking about the two young sisters Kayla and Matty, who went missing a while back. I was sitting on the love seat with my husband, and Jan was sitting on the other couch. "Dang, they still haven't found those sisters!" I yelled. "They've been missing for ages! Since I was a teenager."

"Yeah, they've been missing for a long time. It's very obvious that foul play was involved."

"Don't say that, Courtney! They may be alive somewhere."

"Those young ladies have been missing for years. They would have found them by now."

"I just don't like the thought of them being murdered and their bodies lying in a ditch somewhere."

***

The next day, we went to the grocery store like Courtney said. When we were in the check-out line, something happened that made me wanna slap the taste out of somebody's mouth. It got pretty wild, but thanks to security and my husband, the situation got under control. Courtney had to go back and get some bread, and Jan and I stayed in line so we wouldn't lose our spot. The store was busy. A guy came up to me who appeared to be intoxicated. "What's up mommy? How you doing?" he said, as he stumbled his way towards me.

"Do I know you?" I asked. My daughter stepped closer to me, as if I was gonna leave her.

"No, but you can get to know me though. What's your name?" I was disgusted. The guy could barely talk. The line was moving fast, and we were the next ones to check out.

"Excuse me, but I have to check out." He stepped closer to me, and I was getting angry.

"Come on baby, don't be like that.", he said. That was it, I just lost it and snapped off.

Listen, asshole, if you don't get the hell away from me, we're gonna have some serious problems!"

"Oh, it's like that, huh?"

"Yeah, just like that." I turn around and started to put the items on the conveyer belt. That was when I felt his hands on my butt. I turned around and slapped the heck out of him. I felt like I was the old vicious Ailina off her medication. I wanted to hit him again but I had to remember who I am in Christ. Courtney came back just in time before the guy could do anything else. He pulled me back and said,

"Is there a problem here?"

"Honey, he touched me on my butt, and I slapped him!"

"Is this your girlfriend?" the guy asked.

"No, she's my wife you pinhead! What's the big idea touching my wife like that asshole!"

"Whatcho gonna do homie?" Courtney unbuttoned his shirt and said,

"You wanna go outside and find out Punk bitch!" The security guard came over to help with the altercation.

"What's going on over here?" he asked.

"This drunk pervert sexually assaulted me!"

"No, I didn't. This lady slapped me for no reason!"

I didn't have to say anything because all the other shoppers around me stood up and vouched for me, including the cashier. The security guard escorted him out of the store. He was trying to get Courtney to come outside with him to fight. I told my husband it wasn't worth it. He was drunk anyway. Courtney would have killed that guy. I aways knew my husband didn't play about his virtuous woman. That whole scene was just crazy. I thought my husband was gonna seriously hurt that guy.

***

A week passed by, and things were still looking good for us. I finished the dress for Sue's daughter. She was very grateful, and so was her daughter. My business was doing very well. I had to fire one of my store managers because she was treating the employees like dirt. I got a letter from an employee at the store saying that she was swearing at them and kept screwing up on the hours that they've worked. In the letter, I was told that she was showing favoritism towards other employees. I also got a letter from dozens of customers saying how rude she was. So, I went down to the store and let her go. The assistant manager of the store was then promoted to the store general manager. After that ordeal, things were back to running smoothly at the store. I kept an eye out on it every once in a while. I even made frequent visits.

After a powerful church service on Sunday, things got really heated. Pastor Motesso gave a powerful message, my husband and the praise team did their thing, and I was teaching the kids down in the children's ministry.

That whole day was just fine until we put Jan to bed and went to bed ourselves. Things got all bad. I thought one of us was gonna be dead for sure. "Courtney, are you sleepy?" I asked. As I was laying on his chest.

"No, not really." He turned on his side and put his arms around me. I loved it when he did that. He always felt so warm. I got on top of him and said,

"Let's play." Then I took off my nightgown and unsnapped my bra and pulled it off. My breast was revealed to him. After that I held my head down and kissed him, slipping him the tongue. He started rubbing and touching me all over. Then, we heard the sound of breaking glass downstairs. Courtney pushed me off him and reached for his gun in the nightstand drawer.

"Follow behind me, and when I say so, run to Jan's room. When you get there grab Jan and hide in the closet," Courtney whispered.

I hurried up and put on my pink bathrobe and did as commanded. I held on to the back of his shirt and clenched tightly behind him. He held the gun up in a position as if he was a member of the SWAT team getting ready to break down a door and arrest a criminal. When we made it out of the room, he very softly said, "Go, now."

I ran to my baby's room and woke her up. "Jan, Jan get up baby! Come with mommy!" she took a stretch and said,

"Where are we going mommy?" I didn't answer. I was too startled and shook up. I just grabbed her and ran into the closet. "Mommy, it's dark in here," Jan cried.

"Shhhh, just wait for daddy and stay quiet, honey." I was shaking so bad I could have had a heart attack.

I heard some voices downstairs but couldn't make out the words. The voices seem to be going on for about five minutes. Those were the longest five minutes of my life. Then I heard the scariest sound ever, a gun fire. I screamed so loud Jan got startled and screamed too out of terror. Footsteps began to pound on the stairs. They were getting closer and closer. How did the intruder know we were in the closet? And why did he shoot my husband? He must have heard the cries and the screams. Finally, the footsteps reached the closet door. My heart was beating extremely fast. I was thinking to myself, *I hope he'll just spare my daughter and just take me.* slowly, the door began to open. The shadow of a man stood before us. I screamed loud as I could.

CHAPTER 10
Bad Choice

Finally, the door opened all the way, and a man's voice said, "It's me baby! It's only me." it was Courtney. I got up off the floor and grabbed him tight.

"Oh my God, Courtney, what happed I thought you were shot. I heard the gun go off and everything!"

"I shot him. I had to."

We called the police and moments later, two squad cars pulled up. There were two officers in both cars. It was later on when we went downstairs that I found out that it was the account manager who my husband fired. He came to our house to seek revenge on Courtney. He came with a gun and was prepared to take out my husband.

When we went downstairs, I saw the body of a tall black male with blue jeans on and a white tank top muscle shirt. I grabbed my daughter and shield her eyes. I didn't want her to see that. One of the officers took the guy's pulse and discovered he was still alive. Immediately, an ambulance was called to the scene. We were ordered to wait outside. It was a humid night; lights were flashing everywhere. We explained how we heard broken glass, which was from the living room window next to the front door. Courtney explained to the cops that he knew the guy and once fired him. "Would you mind coming down to the station, sir?" One of the officers said. I looked at Courtney, and he looked back at me. "You're not under arrest. We just need you to come down to the station and make a written statement. You are familiar with the Florida stand your ground law, right?"

"Yes," said Courtney. "Sure, I'll make a written statement." Before Courtney left, he ordered me to call my Grandparents, take Jan, and stay at their house until everything was settled. I gave him a look of concern. I wanted to go with him. "Everything is gonna be ok baby. I'll call you in a little while you have your phone?"

"No, it's in the bedroom." The officers let Courtney escort me back in the house and into the bedroom because I was scared. I put on some clothes and grabbed my phone and car keys. I called my grandparents and gave them the scoop.

Back outside, I put Jan in my car. It was parked in our driveway. The EMS unit was putting the suspect's wounded body in the ambulance. I gave my husband a kiss. He then leaned down in the car and told Jan, "Daddy's gonna be okay, Honey. Don't worry. Okay sweetheart?"

She nodded her head up and down. Then he placed a kiss on her cheek and walked to the squad car. Before I got into my car, I heard something weird over in the bushes. I stopped and looked before getting in my car. It sounded like a rodent running away or something. I started to go over there, but I thought that what if it was just a racoon or something. I just got in my car and drove off.

***

I made it over my grandparents' house, and they were more shaken up than I was. It was about one O'clock the morning. I put my daughter back to sleep and laid her down in my old room. I never saw my baby so startled. She didn't know what was going on, but I could tell she knew it wasn't good. I sat down at the bedside with her and gently stroke her hair with my fingers. I thought about the way my mom used to do that to me. It made me shed a tear. I was already missing my husband. I could just imagine the terror my daughter might be feeling. I felt bad for her. I cried even harder. My grandmother came into the room and sat next to me on the bed. "Are you okay dear?" she asked.

"Yes, I just miss my mom and dad."

"I know you do. How's my grandbaby Jan?"

"She seems to be doing fine now. I just hope my husband is okay."

"Oh, I'm sure he is. He didn't do anything wrong. He had the right to protect his family. The stand your ground law applies in this case." That gave me hope. She had a point. Anxiety was building up in me again. I couldn't wait for Courtney's phone call. I wondered what questions they were asking him. I wanted to know it all. I fell asleep with my baby for a few hours. I woke up to a phone call. It was finally my husband. "Baby... baby are you okay?" I asked.

"Yea, I'm fine sweetheart." He sounded tired. I could hear the scratching in his voice.

"Are you ready to come home, honey?"

"Yea, I told the detectives that I would have you come and pick me up. Is that okay?"

"Of course, I'll come get you."

It was in the middle of the night. I wondered if he wanted to go back home after that whole incident. My grandmother told me to let Jan stay the night since she was sleeping so well. I agreed. I drove down to the police station. Courtney told me all about it. the story that Courtney told them checked out. Apparently, the guy who Courtney fired tried to seek revenge, only it backfired on him. Courtney also told me about the conversation they were having while I was upstairs hiding in Jan's closet.

When Courtney fired him, his wife filed for divorce. She was planning to take everything, even the kids. It was unclear how the guy found our house. I guess when you're angry and full of rage, you could do pretty much anything. I left my baby at my grandparents' house because I didn't want to wake her. She had been through enough already for the night, and what a night that was.

Apparently, the guy lived. He was charged with breaking and entering and having a weapon illegally. I was just happy we were all okay. Anything could have happened to us that night. We kept Jan in the room with us at night for a while. When things like that happen, as a child, it's hard to forget when you get older. She was still a little frantic. Courtney and I comforted her the best way we could, reassuring her that the man was put away and he couldn't come back. Eventually she got over the whole thing.

I woke up one morning and went to my garden to pray. Courtney went over to Pastor Motesso's house so they could do some painting at the church. After I was done praying for an hour or an hour and a half, I went back inside to get ready to go to my office. I got my daughter ready to go to my grandparents' house. I picked up my keys and headed for the door when my phone ranged. It was Toa. "Hey Toa. What's up chica?"

"Hey, bestie! What do you have planned today?"

"I was on my way to my office. Why? What's up?"

"That boy keeps bothering me about you. It's kind of annoying. Can you please call him or something, Just to say hi so he can stop bugging me?" I hesitated for a minute. Then I remembered that my husband did say it was okay. So, I said,

"Okay, I'll call him."

"Good. He can leave me the hell alone." I laughed.

"I gotta go chica, hugs and kisses!"

"Okay gurl, hugs and kisses!"

It wasn't until a few days later that I picked up the phone and gave Billy Rogers a call. I was at home with my daughter, and Courtney was out on some business. Before I completed the dial, I had to gather my words and my thoughts together. I hadn't heard from him in ages. A deep voice answered the phone. He didn't sound like Billy, but I assumed it was him. "Hello, is this Billy, Billy Rogers?"

"Indeed, it is. And this is...?"

"Hi, this is Ailina."

"Ailina! Ailina from High school?"

"Yes." I sat down at my kitchen table.

"Oh wow... this is a surprise. I thought you weren't gonna call me! It's great to hear from you! Oh, my goodness, you don't know how excited I am right now."

"Yea, me too. Sandra and Toa told me you we're back in town. So I decided to call you and say hi."

"Thank you, I'm glad you did. Listen, you think we can get together and like... hang out-get coffee or something? It would be great to see you."

I wasn't really sure at first. I was curious about what he looked like. I wanted to know if he got taller, darker etc. so I decided to meet up with him later that day for lunch. When I pulled up to the coffee shop, I saw him sitting at the table outside with a bundle of flowers. He was looking around, trying to spot me. I walked slowly towards him. He finally saw me coming his way. "Oh, my, God, you still look beautiful as can be!" he said. I gotta admit, I blushed hard. He definitely got taller. He was still handsome, and his complexion was the same. He had a low haircut. I loved the black and brown suit he was wearing. It brought out the color of his brown eyes. I immediately had a flashback when I gave him that kiss at that party years ago. I also had a flashback when he took my virginity in the car. Let's just hope history doesn't repeat itself.

We gave each other a hug before we sat down at our table. We met at a coffee shop not too far from my house. We sat outside because the weather was nice-not too hot or too cold. The wind wasn't blowing hard, and there was a nice breeze. He told me that he took a job as a plant manager at a warehouse. He also told me that he was once married. He got divorced a year after he got married. He said that, for some reason, he couldn't get used to her. "Why not?" I asked. He then said that she was just someone he couldn't get used to. I still wasn't clear on what he meant by "couldn't get used to." I just left well enough alone. We talked and talked, getting caught up on each other. I didn't want to tell him the story when I was held captive and treated like a whore. I thought that was embarrassing. He didn't talk the way he used to talk back in high school. He sounded so proper. I thought it was kind of sexy. He reminded me of my husband.

"Can I ask you a question?" he asked. I fixed my gaze on him, curious to find out what it was he was about to ask me.

"Yes."

"Remember when we were at that house party and you were dared to kiss me?" I didn't know why, but for some reason, I felt myself about to get wet between my legs. I chuckled a little bit and said,

"Yes, I remember, why?" I smiled as I said that.

"I want you to know that I thought about that almost every day, even the time when we had sex in the car." Oh man, why did he say that? I had to close my legs tight under the table because my vagina was getting really wet. I tried to play it off by laughing. He was also laughing. The I said,

"How can I ever forget that time?" I was very serious when I said that. I meant that literally.

"That was a great moment for me," he said.

"Oh yeah… and what was so great about that moment?" I asked, being funny.

"The fact that I had sex with one of the prettiest girls in school." He leaned over closer to me and said, "The truth is, Ailina, is that I was gonna ask you to be my girlfriend that next day, but you ended up going to the hospital. That broke my heart. I was so upset and worried about you."

I didn't know how to feel about that. He sounded so sincere. I wondered what would have happened between the two of us if I hadn't tried to kill myself that day. He had me thinking about a lot of things. Would I have been married to him? Would I have even came across that C-Lo punk and be treated like a sex slave? I had a flashback of everything that happened to me after I tried to kill myself that night. I was in a mental institution, locked up in the devil's playground, mistreated and used sexually, and raped. I stared into space for a while. Then he snapped me out of it by saying, "Ailina, are you okay?" I focused my eyes back on him and said yes and took a sip of my coffee.

We continued talking and enjoying ourselves. We spent about an hour and a half just hanging out. He asked me if we could do this again sometime. I agreed to it. The little reunion was a little awkward, but it was still great to see him. I told Toa about the whole date. I told her the questions that he asked me. She thought he was hitting on me. I kind of thought so too. But I didn't tell her what I was thinking.

***

As time passed, Billy and I continued to hang out. Him, Toa, Sandra, and a few of Billie's high school friends all got together and went to dinner at a nice steak house. We had a wonderful time. We were laughing, joking, and reminiscing on the high school days. "Sandra, remember when you were about to fight that one chick in the lunchroom" asked one of the other guys. "What was her name again? Ellen or something like that?"

"Oh, yea, her name was Erica," Sandra answered. "I was gonna take that bitch head off!" We all laughed. The food was awesome. We were all full and ready to call it a night. I picked up my baby from my grandparents' house and headed home.

When I pulled up in my driveway, I noticed someone had been in the bushes because they were all out of place. Leaves were on the ground, and some of the branches were broken. I thought maybe it was Courtney. My baby and I sat on the couch, waiting for my husband to get home from his last-minute meeting with his boss. The time was about seven-thirty, and it was getting dark. The evening news was on, and they were still talking about the two girls who were missing-Kayla and Matty.

Jan fell asleep in my arms, so I went upstairs and put in her bed. I kissed her on her cheek and said, "goodnight munchkin." I went back downstairs and into the kitchen to get a drink of mango juice. Something caught my attention when I looked out my kitchen window into my garden. I noticed my plants were out of whack. I walked out there to investigate. Dirt was on the concrete path, and some petals were all over the place and everything. But the crucial thing I've found, was the cigarette butts by my sunflowers. That was odd because my husband and I didn't smoke. Someone had been in my garden for sure. Minutes later, I heard footsteps creeping up behind me. Then I felt a hand touch my shoulder. It made me jump, and I quickly turned around.

"Sorry baby. I didn't mean to startle you." It was Courtney. I took a deep sigh and hugged him.

"Hi honey," I said. Then I kissed him on his lips.

"Goodness gracious, what did you do to your garden?" he asked.

"I didn't do this. Neither did I put those cigarettes butts there."

Courtney thought it was that guy who he had shot. He thought he might have been stalking our house for days. It made sense, but I still wasn't sure. Courtney helped me clean the mess up. It wasn't like this the last time I was in my garden. I just left it alone.

We continued to do our duties at the church. The ministry was growing. New people were joining. Pastor Motesso was doing an awesome job leading the congregation. We all were very proud of him.

The next day, Billy called me at my office. He asked me if we could get lunch together around noon. I agreed. We went to a local sandwich shop. I had a chicken fillet with fries. He had a Rueben sandwich. We both took an hour break. We continued on and off hanging out with each other. I admit I enjoyed his company. We were friends, until one day, something happened. It was something that changed the course of everything I had going for myself.

One day, Billy asked me if I would like to come to his house for lunch. I told him I would think about it. It took me a while, but I was thinking to myself, *this is just lunch. Nothing is gonna happen.*

I arrived at his house, and I gotta admit, it was a nice dig. It wasn't extremely big, but it was still nice. His brown leather sofa was off the chain though. It also smelled good as ever. It was a Hawaiian tropical smell. He made us chicken alfredo pasta. It was delicious. After a while, I told him I had to get back to my office. He then said, "Thanks for coming over for lunch."

We gave each other a hug. The way he hugged me back was not one of those friendly see-you-later hugs. It was one of those, *please don't leave me because I want you hugs.* He held me so close and tight. I didn't want to let him go. I could tell he didn't want to let me go either. When we slowly drifted apart, our cheeks were touching each other's until we ended up locking lips. He wrapped my arms around his head. His lips were still soft to the touch. My tongue ended up touching his. I felt his hands softly land on my butt. After he sensed that it was okay to do so, he gripped it tightly. I began to moan as he started kissing my neck.

We ended up on his couch and continued to foreplay. He started unbuttoning my shirt as I continued to tongue-kiss him. My black bra was exposed, and he put his hands on my breast. He then started to take off his shirt. My goodness, he had a very nice body. I was so lost in the moment I almost forgot who I was. I unzipped my skirt and I let him pull it off. He climbed between my legs and kissed me some more. I unsnapped my bra, and he began to suck on my breast, nibbling on my nipples. I unbuckled his belt, unbuttoned his pants, and he pulled them off. I took my panties off, and he stuck it in. He put it in inch by inch. It felt good, just as I remembered it. I was enjoying every second of it. He had me moaning loud as he was stroking and pounding. I took control as I got on top of him and started to ride. I couldn't believe what I was doing. It dawned on me that I just had an affair with the guy I lost my virginity to back in high school.

After we were done, I put my clothes back on and headed for the door. Before I left, I made him promise not to tell anyone about what just happened. He agreed. "Will I see you again?" he asked.

"Yea, of course."

I left the house and headed back to my office. I told my front desk secretary not to forward any calls to me, unless it was my husband. I went into my office and closed the door, thinking about what just happened. I was having all kinds of mixed feelings. Why did I enjoy that? What was happening to me? I couldn't believe I still had feelings for him after all those years. Don't get me wrong, I still love my husband and always will.

I checked my messages, and one stood out. I had gotten a message from a modeling company that wanted to use some of my clothing designs on their models. I called them back and arranged a meeting with them. I broke the news to Courtney when we went to dinner that evening. We had our baby with us. He was happy for me. "You hear that, Jan? Mommy is gonna be a star!" he said. She looked at me and gave me the biggest smile ever.

A couple of days later, Toa and Sandra asked me to go get our nails done. The only thing that was on my mind was what Billy and I had done. Part of me couldn't wait to do it again. The other part was saying, *you're dumb as hell. You have a good husband at home and a beautiful daughter. Why mess that up?*

We continued the affair. We had sex almost every opportunity we got-in his kitchen, in the shower, in his car on our lunch break, and even at a local park. I didn't know how long we were gonna do this for. One time, he came to my office for a little while. A month after the affair, the strangest thing happened. It was something that made me regret the choice I had made. It was something that started the biggest nightmare you could ever imagine.

CHAPTER 11
Enemy From The Past

One particular afternoon I met Billy at his house for some afternoon sex. We both were ready to get in on. I joined him in his shower. I lifted my right leg up, and he gave me head. I bent over and he stuck it in me. minutes later, I heard the door bust open. A lady pulled back the shower curtain and yelled, "What the fuck is this!"

"Mandy, what are you doing here?" Billy said.

"Who is this, Billy?" I asked

"No, *bitch,* the question is who the hell are you?" she said. "I'm his wife!" I got out of the shower and wrapped a dry towel around me.

"Billy, I thought you were divorced!"

"No bitch, we're still legally married, honey!" She lifted her left hand up and showed me her ring. I couldn't believe this was happening. I was so pissed. Then I said,

"You call me a bitch again, Imma go to my car, grab my gun, and blow your fuckin' head off! I was serious as a heart attack. She called me a bitch again. So I put my clothes on and headed for the front door to get my gun. Immediately, Billy stopped me. "I thought you were divorced Billy!" I yelled.

"Okay, look, we're not legally divorced. We've been separated for quite some time."

"And you felt you couldn't tell me that!"

"I didn't want to lose you again Li Li!"

"Well, you just did!" I stormed out the door and left in my car.

I was about two seconds away from shooting that girl. She had me all the way messed up. I went back to my office. I waited in my car for a few minutes because I was crying. My mind was all over the place. I didn't want anyone to see in that state I was in. I made the decision to break it off with Billy. After I got myself together, I went up to my office. I was informed by one of my secretaries that my husband called and said that he'd be home at around seven tonight. That gave me an idea. I decided to go back to Billy's house and tell him face-to-face that it was over.

I also made the decision that I was gonna tell Courtney what I had been doing. I just didn't know when. I wish I never got involved with Billy in the first place. I called Toa and told her what had been going on with Billy and I. "Oh my God chica!" A tear was in my eye as I said,

"Please Toa, don't look at me as a hoe. Please don't judge me. I know I messed up really bad. That's why I'm going to his house and breaking it off."

"Hey… girl, I'll never judge you. I love you so much, and I don't want anything to happen to you. You're doing the right thing by breaking it off. I can never judge you or call you a hoe. We've been besties since kindergarten."

She made me feel better. At the end of the day, I grabbed my things and headed to Billy's house. My heart was beating fast. On my way there, I was gathering my thoughts. I had it all thought out. I thought about how I was gonna break the news to my husband. That was gonna be the hardest part. I betrayed him. He deserves to know the truth. He's a good man, by the way. I was truly sorry. I felt so bad and ashamed of myself. If it wasn't for my husband, I would be dead right now.

I finally made it to Billy's house. I took a deep breath. This was gonna be one of the hardest things I'd ever done. I know his heart was gonna be broken. This was for the best. I had to be honest. I loved our little relationship. His sex was off the charts, but now it was time to put an end to the fun. I got out of my car and walked up to his door step. Immediately, something caught my attention. First, the door was wide-open. I stepped slowly inside. Muddy shoe prints were on the carpet, and there was blood on the wall behind his leather couch. My heart dropped after I saw the horrible dead bodies of Billy and his wife, Mandy. There was a message written on the wall with a black marker. It said, *Ailina is a cheater.*

Obviously, someone knew about us. I screamed in terror as I ran out the door. I called 911. Within five minutes, the FBI showed up along with the CSI and the forensics team. They taped off the front and back of the house. I called Toa and Sandra and broke them the news. They came right away. I figured this was all my fault. I never felt so bad in my life. My affair with Billy got him killed. Who in the heck knew about us? Whoever knew must have killed him, but who?

"Are you Ailina, the one who made the discovery, and the one who made the phone call?" asked one of the detectives.

"Yes."

"You mind if I ask you a couple of questions?"

"Sure."

"How did you know the victims?"

"Billy was a friend from high school. The lady, Mandy, who I just met today was his wife. He told me they were still legally married but separated." He began to write down everything I was saying. Because I made the discovery, It was obvious that they knew I knew what was written on the wall. They didn't release that of information to the public, just in case someone blob and say what was actually written. Only the killer would know that information.

"Were you having an affair with the victim?" I answered truthfully. He then went on and asked me if I knew anyone who would want him or his wife dead. He asked me if he had any enemies. I said,

"No, not that I know of." I walked back over to Toa and cried in her arms. I was so sad. This was the same feeling I felt when my parents and Mia died. I called my husband and asked him to please meet me at home. He was in a meeting. I told him that it was an emergency, and I really needed to talk to him. He agreed. I told Toa and Sandra; I would call them later.

Surprisingly, Courtney beat me home. I ran in the house and into his arms. "What's wrong baby?" I literally couldn't talk for a minute.

"Can you just hold me!", I said. He held me tightly.

"Baby, you're scaring me, what's going on! Talk to me." I was trying to catch my breath and calm myself down. I took deep breaths and calmly told him what happened.

"Okay, do you remember my friend I was telling you about, the one who moved back in town?"

"Yea, remember, why?"

"He was murdered today."

"What!"

"Along with his wife."

"Holy crap! What kind of madman would do such a thing!"

"I saw the bodies in his house." He looked at me with confusion and said,

"Wait… wait, what? What do you mean in his house?"

"Can you sit down for a second?" He yelled and said,

"No, I'm sitting down. you're gonna tell me what's going on, and you're gonna tell me right now!" I felt my body temperature rising. I was so scared, so I just let it all out at once

"I've been sleeping with him for the past month. Someone found out and killed him!"

"WHAT THE FUCK AILINA! How could you do that! I can't believe you!" I trusted you, I fucking trusted you!"

"I KNOW, BABY, AND I'M SORRY. I'M SO SORRY! Please don't be mad!"

"Don't be mad! What the fuck you mean don't be mad! You have no idea how I feel right now!" I walked toward him and tried to hold him. He stopped me and pushed me back. "Don't you fucking, touch me! How could you do this to me, Ailina! To us! Our daughter! We got a good thing going for ourselves, and you just gonna fuck it up! Tell me something, when you were fucking him, did you ever think about the time I saved your life? DID YOU!" I was crying so hard. "I've been nothing but a blessing to you. Never have I thrown that in your face!"

"I know baby, I know and I love you for that. Please believe me, I didn't mean to hurt you!"

"You just told me you've been fucking him for a month! Were you thinking about me at all? Huh? Were you thinking about my feelings? ANSWER ME!"

"Yes! I was!"

"You wanna know how I know you're lying? Because you would have never slept with him in the first place. Now you got him killed! I feel bad for the guy. I bet he wasn't a bad person." I was feeling all the guilt and shame. He made me feel so low and guilty, and I couldn't stand myself at that moment.

"Courtney, you have no idea how bad I feel right now. I didn't mean for any of this to happen!" Tears were just running down my face like a waterfall.

"Fuck you, Ailina! FUCK YOU!"

"Please don't say that Courtney, you don't mean that." He flipped the table over and yelled again,

"FUCK YOU!" My heart just sank at that moment, I felt that he didn't love me anymore. I felt like I was in another dimension, like I had died and went to hell, only without fire.

"Courtney, I love you, I love you with all my heart!"

"No, the fuck you don't because if you did, you wouldn't have done some stupid-ass shit like this. You know what's really sad somebody died because of your fuckup!"

"Courtney, please give me the benefit of the doubt. I know I messed up, and I admit that, but please don't give up on me, don't give up in us!"

"Us? There was never no us! I'm done with you!" he grabbed his keys off the couch and headed for the door. I ran behind him.

"Courtney… Courtney wait! You don't mean this. Please don't leave me. lets work this out! I grabbed the back of his shirt. He turned around and pushed me on the floor. I just laid there, crying. Before he left, he said,

"I had a surprise for you, but I guess it's pointless to show you now." He closed the door behind him and left.

I was on the floor crying so hard that I threw up. My husband had just left me, and I got a good friend killed today. I didn't know how to go on. I couldn't live with myself. I went upstairs and grabbed a gun, then ran in the bathroom. First, I looked in the mirror. The tears were flowing down my face. I didn't see myself as a woman of God anymore. I saw myself as a whore and a cheater. I held the gun to my head ready to pull the trigger. My old suicide thoughts were coming back. My hand was shaking uncontrollably. I had tried to kill myself before, maybe this time I will be successful. I had failed in my marriage, I failed my daughter, and most of all, I failed my Lord God.

Right when I was about to pull the trigger, I thought about what my mother had said to me a long time ago. She said, "Anytime I feel I messed up or did something terrible, I just go in my garden and pray, seek forgiveness from the Lord."

I thought about that. I thought about my baby. Courtney had left me now; all I had was my daughter. I put the gun down and walked outside to my garden. I prayed to God. I prayed hard and long, crying at the same time.

"Father, I'm sorry. Please forgive me I forgive everyone who ever harmed me in any way. Please bring my husband back to me. put it in his heart to forgive me. I'm sorry for Billy and his wife, God. I just want everything to go back to normal. Please, God, take this pain away from me."

I continued for a while. I prayed until I couldn't pray no more. When I was done, I was about to go out and look for my husband. I walked back to the door. All of a sudden, I felt a hard blow to the back of my head. I hit the ground, and then it was lights out for me.

***

As I was regaining consciousness, I felt that my mouth was covered with something. My arms were tied behind my back, and I was sitting in a seat. From the movement, I could tell I was in a car, and the car was in motion. I had no idea what the heck was going on. Did my own husband knock me out and abducted me? everything was blurry at first until, I slowly, things came back to focus. I heard a familiar male voice say, "Well, hello there sweetness. I see you're finally awake." I turned my head to see who it was. When I finally recognized the voice and the face, I got so scared and chills went down my spine. "Did you miss me? I surely missed you." He ripped the tapped off my mouth.

"C-Lo… how did you find me?" I asked. I couldn't believe it was him.

"It wasn't that hard my dear. When you become the boss of your own company, you can make yourself a target. I even have one of your business cards."

"What do you want? Where are you taking me?"

"What I want is revenge. That was really clever of you. Crashing the car and escaping. What some guts you have. Looks like you're going to your grave." I started shaking. I was so scared. I just knew I was about to die. I guess this was my punishment for my wrongdoings.

"I had to escape from you. You treated me like a whore and a punching bag! What did you expect me to do!"

"Looks like you're still a whore. I've been watching you, Ailina. I've been watching you longer than you think. You have a beautiful kid by the way. Too bad you're not gonna see her grow up. Her name is Jan, right?"

"How did you know that?"

"Like I said, I've been watching you, stalking your house for a very long time." It finally hit me. he was the one I'd been hearing in my bushes. He was the one who left those cigarettes in my garden, knocking over my plants and spreading petals everywhere. Everything was making sense to me. I had no idea it was him. He was supposed to be long gone out of my life. Now he was back with a vengeance.

"C-Lo, please, I'm a totally different woman now. I'm a child of God. I'm not who I used to be."

"Is that right, miss I wanna cheat on my husband!" you surely seem like the same hoe to me." I got mad and said,

"FUCK YOU!" That was when he reached over and slapped me. He opened up the console of his car and pulled out a nine-millimeter handgun. I got so scared I almost pissed myself. I felt like I was in a horror movie and was being taken to a secret layer to be eaten by monsters. He also pulled out a bottle of whiskey and started drinking it.

So, my arms were tied behind my back and C-Lo was drinking while driving, getting drunk. On top of that, he had a gun ready to kill me. He went on saying how he followed me almost every day. He told me how he was there when that guy came to our house, trying to kill my husband. He said he was hiding in the bushes. That explained the sound I've heard when we were leaving.

"Your husband is no joke when it comes to his family," he said. "He really did a number on that clown. Truth is, I was gonna kill that coward before he got to you. Thanks to your husband, he did the job for me. sorry about the garden. I find your garden to be a very peaceful place." He just went on and on about my garden. He told me he was infatuated with it. he said his favorite plants in the garden are the purple violets, but what he said next sent chills up my spine. It was like everything was coming together piece by piece.

"That jerk Billy had it coming!" I looked at him with a look of confusion. Was he about to tell me that he killed Billy and his wife? "Who the hell did he think was-fucking my lady, having lunch with her and shit!" He took another sip of his whiskey.

"Did you kill him?" I asked.

"Indeed, him and his wife. She was collateral damage. Can't leave witnesses now can I." I gave him a look that a dog will make when they are in attack mode. Then I said,

"Prove it. I don't believe you!"

"That's easy to prove. I wrote Ailina is a cheater on the wall with a black marker. I shot them both in the head." I don't know what came over me, but I got mad as hell. I started screaming from the top of my lungs and wiggling my arms to get free.

"YOU SON OF A BITCH, UNTIE ME RIGHT NOW!" He started laughing like it was funny. I couldn't believe he just laughed. No regard for human life. I was beyond angry. "You didn't have to kill him!"

"Oh yes, of course I did he had no business with another man's wife anyway. In fact, I told you before, if I can't have you, then no one will."

"In that case, why didn't you kill my husband?"

"I could have, but when I saw who he was, I couldn't do it. That Billy boy though, I had to give it to him." I gave him the meanest look I can give him and said,

"You, asshole!" he slapped me again.

He continued to drive. I had no idea where we were going. It was dark as ever. There were no streetlights. It had been just over forty-five minutes, and I was getting nervous by the second. He kept going on and on about how he would follow me back and forth from my home and to my office. It was very creepy if you ask me. I was just disgusted. It made me sick to my stomach. He held me hostage in his home, stalked me for months, killed Billy, and now he was kidnapping me. I thought for a minute, *I escaped once, I can do it again.* This time, he tied my hands behind my back, so I couldn't grab the stirring wheel again. It took God almighty to help me get out of this one.

CHAPTER 12

Dangerous Girl

We drove for about an hour and a half before he made a left turn, going deeper and deeper into a wooded area. There were lots of trees, bushes, and large tree trunks that had fallen over from previous storms. He stopped the car and put it in park. Then he took a cigarette out of his pocket and started smoking. "What are you gonna do with me?" I asked. He took a puff and just stared at me. "What are you gonna do with me?"

"First, I'm gonna get drunk. Then, we're gonna make love, just like the old times." It sounded like he was intending on raping me. He got out of the car and stumbled over to the passenger side. He opened the door and untied me. I started swinging and kicking at him until he punched me in the face, knocking me out. It felt like the whole car was spinning. I was out cold.

I woke up in the back of the car with my clothes half off my body. My shirt was torn off, and I had no idea where my skirt was. C-Lo pulled my panties up and dragged me out of the car. Then he pulled the gun out, picked me up by my hair, put the gun to my head and ordered me to walk. As we were walking, he had a tight grip on the back of my neck. We walked deeper and deeper into the woods. He was slapping me and kicking me whenever I fell to the ground. I was in a lot of pain. My feet starting hurting because I'd been walking with no shoes on.

"Before I kill you, I want to show you something. I've never shown anyone this, so you should feel special. I've been waiting forever to get this out. I can show you because you're about to die anyway." I felt like a prisoner being led to the electric chair for execution, like I was taking the last walk. My knees got weak, and I fell again. I didn't want to walk anymore. I just dropped to the ground.

"Please… don't kill me! I'll do anything you want! Just name it." I was crying and pleading for my life.

"You know what I want darling, revenge! When you crashed that car, I suffered a broken nose. No one ever did that to me before. Now you gonna pay!" He kicked me after he said that. Then he picked me up and slapped me so hard blood flew out of my mouth. I fell down and balled my whole body up in a fetus position. He started laughing and said, "Aww, look at the little lady. What's wrong, my dear? You can't get up?" I started to scream as loud as I could, "HELP! SOMEONE PLEASE HELP ME!"

He started laughing again. Then he said, "Do you know where we are, sweetheart? You can scream all you want. There's no one around here. We are over eighty miles away from the city parts of Florida, well away from civilization. We're deep in the woods. Screaming is pointless, honey." Well, that was just my luck. "Now get the fuck up and start walking before I shoot you!"

I slowly got up and started walking. Every step I took, I thought to myself, *I'm getting steps closer to dying.* I thought about how I would never see my daughter and my husband again. I thought about my grandparents and how I treat them when I was a teenager. My feet were killing me, and I was stepping on pinecones, rocks and sticks. I noticed that the alcohol he consumed was finally getting to him, so I hatched another plan to get away. I put the plan into action.

I fell to the ground on purpose. Then I told him I couldn't go on because I had something stuck in my foot. He leaned down, and that was when I kicked him in his nose since it was once broken. I got up and ran as fast as I could. Seconds later, I heard the sound of gunshots. I ran like my life depended on it because it literally did.

***

I tripped over a log and quickly got back up. The sound of his voice screaming my name indicated he was on my trail. He shot more bullets my way, trying to shoot me. After a while, I was running out of stamina. I had to get somewhere and hide to regain my strength and stamina. I saw a huge tree a couple of feet from a little swamp area. I ran behind it and sat down, trying to catch my breath. It smelled so horrible around there. It smelled like dead rodents.

"Ailina, come out, come out, where ever you are." I covered my mouth because I was breathing so hard, and I didn't want him to hear me. I slowly peeked around the tree, and saw him pointing the gun, looking around trying to spot me. He kept yelling my name, telling me to come out. More shots were fired for intimidation. After he fired the whole clip, he reloaded. When I heard no more gunshots and thought he was nowhere in sight, I took off and started running again.

I had no idea where I was running to, but I just ran until I couldn't run anymore. I saw a large tree knocked over on the ground. I decided to sit down and catch my breath again. About five minutes went by, and there was still no sign of C-Lo. I thought I was free until I was grabbed from behind and dragged off the fallen tree. "Hi Ailina, nice to see you again. You just keep pushing my fuck-you-up button aren't you!"

I screamed in horror. I couldn't believe he had found me again. Looks like we were back to where we started. When was this nightmare gonna end. "C-Lo, please… just let me go! I promise I won't go to the police!" He slapped me again. I had blood all over me. This time, he dragged me all the way to the final destination. We came to a little shed. It had tree roots growing on it. the smell inside was just awful. It smelled so bad that I threw up. What I saw inside was the reason why it smelled so bad. It was a very horrible scene. There were two human skulls and skeleton remains. You could tell whoever those two people were, they had been dead for years.

"You see those skeletons? Take a good look at what happens to girls who leave me. they were my hoes. They both decided to leave me at the same time. These two sisters had it coming. Their names were Matty and Kayla." I was in a state of shock. The two young ladies who had been missing were actually dead, and this sick bastard killed them. I got so sad and I started crying. Poor girls.

"So you were the one who killed them," I said softly and angrily."

"I had to. I shot both of them in the head, right where you're standing. Kayla was the brave one. She kind of reminds me of you-always fighting, you know. That's why I had to kill her first. She tried to protect her sister but failed. I blame her for the murders. At the end of the day, she ended up getting both of them killed."

He went on about how he had kidnapped them, like he did me. He told me detail by detail the whole thing. First, he said he put both of them in the trunk of his car and drove all the way up here. Then he said Kayla kept begging him not to kill her sister. She wanted him to kill her and let Matty go. He pointed the gun and was about to shoot Matty first. Kayla tried to stop him by grabbing the gun. He overpowered her and shot her in the head. Matty screamed, and he shot her next.

I could just imagine the horror and fear those two girls were feeling at that time. Something came over me again. I was no longer scared. Hearing that story gave me strength. I had so much respect for Kayla as she was trying to protect her sister. Her bravery struck something in me. The last straw was what he said next. "I once hit a little girl with my car." My eyes got big as I thought about Mia. Then I questioned him,

"How long ago was that?"

"That had to be, I don't know may almost twenty years ago or something," he replied. Yep, that was around the same time Mia was struck by a car. He even said it looked like she was crossing the street to play with some other little girl. I balled my fist up really tight. Very calmly I said,

"That little girl you've killed, was my childhood friend. Her name was Mia-Mia Longwell." He said he had been drunk that day-dunk like he is now. The son of a bitch killed my friend and had no remorse for anything he had done. I was no longer Ailina who was a woman of God. I turned back in to Ailina who was dangerous-the Ailina who was once in a mental institution for trying to kill someone. I was that evil *bitch* again, Ailina the dangerous girl.

Inside I felt like I had to avenge the deaths of those girls and Mia. He had never met that side of me before. The bastard was about to meet the real Ailina- the dangerous woman alive. He had too much liquor. That was the advantage I had over him. He cocked his gun and said,

"Okay, Ailina, it's time for you to go off to the next world." He pointed the gun at me. I wasn't scared one little bit. "When you get to heaven, tell Kayla and Matty I said hi. Oh yea... and tell Mia she shouldn't have been in the street."

That was it. I charged at him and tried to grab the gun. There was a struggle for a brief moment. The gun went off once, striking a tree. I managed to punch him in his eye. He dropped the gun, and because it was so dark, I didn't see where it had fallen. He was so drunk he couldn't even stand straight. Even though he was much older and stronger than me, he couldn't keep up because he was drunk. We exchanged blows. I was swinging with all my might. He tried to grab me because he was losing balance. He wasn't gonna strike fear in me or anyone else anymore. He surely wasn't gonna kill me like Matty and Kayla.

The battle continued as he somehow got me on the ground. I was trying my hardest not to let him on top of me. He managed to do so. "YOU ABOUT TO DIE NOW BITCH!" He yelled.

"Let me up! Let me up you fucking coward! I yelled back. He then said,

"Not until your dead!" He took his hands and placed them around my neck, trying to choke me. What I did was used my legs to scoot closer to the stone I saw not too far from me. I grabbed it and struck him on the head with it. Then I was able get from under him and catch my breath because he had been choking me. I had a chance to run again, but not this time. I wanted to fight him, and fight I did. As he was rolling around on the ground, holding his head, I ran over and kicked him, saying,

"Come on! Come on, you bastard!" I realized that I wasn't' doing much damage because I was still barefooted.

When he got back up, we were exchanging blows again. His hits weren't having much effect on me. The alcohol played a huge role in that. I scratched and clawed his face every time he grabbed me. what a battle this was. It was like an action movie where the good and bad guy had to square off the settle the score. I was determined to avenge the death Kayla, Matty, Billy, and Mia. This world wasn't big enough for the two of us. One of us had to go, and it wasn't gonna be me.

My bra was torn off; blood was coming from my mouth and nose. I had scratches and bruises all over my body, and I was still fighting. "You will never win this fight!" he said.

"That's what you think!" I replied. Then I said, "Bring that shit on over here again punk bitch!"

He put me in a head lock and I bit his nipple as hard as I could. He screamed and let me go. When he let me go, I gave him a nice punch to the face. That was a good one because he stumbled back a few feet. He gave me one back, and I fell because I slipped on something hard. He picked up a nice size log and was about to hit me with it. Luck was on my side as I realized what I had stepped on was the gun that had fallen. I picked it up and shot him twice in his chest. He fell to the ground. I got up and hovered over him with the gun and said,

"Don't move! You move, and I'll blow your fucking head off! Right here!"

"You ca… can't kill me," he said, struggling to talk. "You're not… you're not a killer Ailina!"

"You have no idea what I'm capable of right now. I forgot to tell you, this girl you see before you, were once institutionalized for trying to kill someone. I almost did. I'm the dangerous girl you never wanted to meet." He started coughing up blood. "Who the hell do you think you are-killing those girls, Killing Billy, running over my friend, doing all those horrible things to me!"

"What are you gonna do Ailina, kill me?"

"Indeed I am." I shot him in the leg, and he screamed,

"Ahhh, shit! Okay! Okay! Look let's make a deal, alright! Let's make a deal!" I was curious about what he had to say.

"I'm listening." I slowly lowered the gun but was still on my guard. He coughed up more blood and said,

"I… I'll turn myself in."

I thought about that. Justice for those girls would be alright with me. Besides, when convicted, he would be sentenced to death anyway. This was a win and win situation. I already won the battle. Now I was about to win the war. But then I thought about something. There was no forensic evidence against him. There was no guarantee that he would even turn himself in. because of his background, I knew he couldn't be trusted. "I got a better idea. I'll let you live if you show me the way out of these woods. Then you can crawl your way back."

He used the tree that was behind him to lift himself on his feet. That's when I pointed the gun at him again. "How the hell do you get out of here?" He said it was a straight shot and pointed to my right. My plan was to let him rot in these woods. I started to walk. Seconds later, I heard him trying to hop toward me with a log. I turned around and shot him in the stomach. He fell to the ground.

"Wait, w… wait! He yelled. "Do… Do… Don't kill me. Just hear… hear me out. P… please." Now what did he have to say? "I… I wasn't always like this," he said, struggling to talk.

He went on and told me the tale of how he used to be a good kid. He said he grew up with an abusive father. His dad used to beat him and his mother. All his life, he was raised around violence. C-Lo had no real positive male role models in his life as a child. All the male figures he grew up around were pimps, drug dealers, gangbangers, and even murders. He also told me the gruesome tale of how he sat and watched his dad murder his mom in the kitchen. His dad was sentenced to death and executed years ago.

"You see Ailina, this… this isn't my fa… fought! I wish… I wish my life could have been different." I still had the gun pointed to him. "I… I'm sorry… for all I did. You think I…" he coughed up blood again. Then continued. "You think I wanted to be this person! Well, I didn't!"

I had a flashback of Mia getting hit; him killing Kayla, Matty, Billy. And all those horrible things he did to me. Nothing else he could have said would have stopped me from killing him. He wasn't talking to Ailina the woman of God. She would have forgiven him. He was talking to Ailina the dangerous girl. I emptied the rest of the clip in his chest. I did exactly what I wanted to do. I avenged all the murders that he committed. He stopped talking, he stopped moving, and then he stopped breathing, that, was the end of C-Lo.

***

Wow, I've just killed someone. I gotta admit that felt good. He would never be able to hurt anyone else again. The word is that you reap what you sow. I didn't care about his childhood-how he was raised or none of that trash. The only thing that was sad to me was how he saw his mother get murdered by his dad. I could now see where he got his violence from. So, he was now dead, and I had to find my way out of these woods.

I had no idea where I was at. I looked around on the ground to find my shirt that got torn off. I was able to find it. The shirt was so messed up I had to just tie it around my breast. It was very humid and dry. The darkness made it very hard for me to see where I was going. There were mist and fog everywhere as well. I just walked and walked until I came to an open road.

I was scared as ever. I still had the nine-millimeter handgun. Even though it was emptied, I still kept it, just in case I needed to beat off wild creatures. The sound of crickets and owls were getting to me. I was just hoping I didn't hear any wolves. My body started to ache from the battle. My feet were getting blisters on them. I took off the torn shirt and ripped it in half. Then I tied each half on my two feet. This was gonna be a long night. Mother nature could be scary sometimes. On the other hand, she could be your best friend, if you know how to treat her. Nocturnal creatures love to come out night. Some even love wooded areas.

There were little chipmunks running all over the place. Every step I took made my body ache. I was so sore from that fight. The fog was making it hard for me to see what was ahead. It had to be at least past one O'clock a.m. It looked like I wasn't gonna make it to the open road anytime soon. I had a long way to go. The hot humidity was making me dehydrated. I needed water badly, especially from the battle I was just in.

When I looked up at the sky, I saw the beautiful stars. There was a full moon, and I believed I had seen a bat fly past it. I continued my journey out of the woods. Suddenly, I saw a possum come out of a huge log. It was big as hell. I thought it was a huge rat at first. It just looked at me. Immediately, I gripped the barrow of the gun, ready to hit it, just case it tried to attack me. The creature just sniffed around, looking for food.

I started getting bitten by mosquitos. Because I was so exposed, they were able to bite me everywhere. I just had to get the hell out of these woods. The only light around was coming from the bright moon. After a while, I started to see fireflies. I was definitely in a twilight zone. I continued to walk and walk. An owl stared at me from a tree that was in front of me. Its eyes were wide-open. It was staring at me like it was waiting on me to leave. It then flew down toward the ground. I thought it was gonna attack me, but it swooped down and snatched a chipmunk and flew off into the midnight sky.

It seemed as though I was walking for hours. My body began to get weaker and weaker. I needed water. Crickets continued to sound, and the creatures of the night roamed about. I saw bugs I had never seen before, heard sounds I've never heard, and some more stuff. Man, I was a total mess.

My breasts were exposed, and I only had on panties and a shirt tied around my feet. I had dead leaves in my hair, and I was dirty as a hobo.

I came to a small river creek. Part of me wanted to take a drink. The water didn't look bad, until I saw a dead racoon floating in it. I sat down to take a little rest a tree stump. I didn't have to worry about C-Lo because I put him out of his misery. Less than five minutes later, I felt something crawling up my leg. When I looked down, I saw that it was huge spider. I quickly jumped up and swiped it off me. It was like nowhere was safe in the woods. I had to get out of there soon.

So, I walked and walked until I came to what seemed like a plain open grass field and a security fence about almost eighty yards away, so I started walking. Right away, I knew there had to be an open road somewhere. The moment I saw the fence, my attention was fixed on two red wolves approaching me. I immediately ran toward the fence. They were hot on my trail, barking and growing, as if I was little red riding hood. That was the fastest I'd ever ran. I think I reached the fence in a matter of seconds, less than a minute. Apparently, the fence was put there to keep out wild creatures. I dropped the gun and climbed up on the fence. I climbed. Fast as I could. The wolves tried to jump up and grab my leg, but I was already too high to reach. When I reached the top, I just paused to catch my breath and then jumped down to the other side of the fence.

I continued the journey down the road, stumbling half naked, bloody, tits showing, and dehydrated. I walked for hours and hours, not knowing if I was going the right way or not. The sun began to rise. I guessed the time had to be between five and six in the morning. Out of breath, tired, sleepy, dehydrated, and starving, my body just gave out I hit the ground. It was lights out again.

CHAPTER 13

Recovery

What a nightmare that was. I won the fight against C-Lo. He killed Billy, kidnapped me; then confessed to killing the two sisters, Matty and Kayla, and running over Mia. On top of that I had to find my way out of the woods. The spirit of God must have had his angels camped about me for sure that night. I could have been dead, and no one would have found my body.

I woke up to the sound of beeping noises and people talking loudly outside the room. There was an IV inside of me. It didn't take me long to realize I was in a hospital. "Oh, my lord, you're awake!" said a soft and familiar voice. I turned my head to see who it was. It was my grandmother. She placed her hand on mine and said, "Are you okay, dear?" with a scratchy voice and could barely talk I said,

"Gra… grandma… I'm so ha…happy to see you!" she rubbed her fingers through my hair. I loved it when she did that.

"How are you feeling honey?"

"Horrible."

"Aww, sweety." My voice was slowly coming back. I cleared my throat and said,

"Are you here by yourself grandma?"

"No, your husband, Courtney and your granddad are here. They went to the cafeteria to get something to eat. They took Jan with them." I was so happy to hear that. The question was, *had Courtney forgiven me?*

"How did I get here?" I asked.

"You were picked up off the road from a family coming back from a camping trip. When they found you, you were in bad shape. Courtney reported you missing. When you arrived here, we were asked to come and see if we could make a positive identification by detectives. What happened to you? How did you end up over hundreds of miles from the city?" Courtney and my grandfather came back in the room with my baby.

"Ailina! Baby, are you alright?" Courtney said, as he ran over to my bed and hugged me. I hugged him back, crying at the same time. Then my daughter jumped in the bed and hugged me.

One of the nurses came in when she heard I was awake. She was middle-age with goldish-blond hair. She also had a few gray strands. Her eyes were gray, and she had a sweet, innocent voice. "Hi, Mrs. Maynord," she said. "I'm nurse Amelia. I see you're finally up."

"How long have I been here?" I asked.

"Less than two days. You were very dehydrated. We had to place an IV in you to put the fluids back in your body. You were very banged up. You also had lots of head trauma." She then continued to read from the chart in her hand. "According to our records, you had a concussion. We had to give you special ointment for your blistered feet." She then told me that a detective would like to speak to me about what took place. That was when it was time. It was time to tell the story of how I was abducted and had the battle of the century.

Two agents came in and sat next to me. One of them was a heavy-set black man with a gray mustache. The other one was a younger-looking white male. He had facial hair, and the hair on his head was ear length. The heavyset black officer whipped out his badge and said, "Hello, Mrs. Maynord. I'm detective Stewart, and this is my partner, Agent Doran. We just wanna know what happened. If you don't mind us asking you about what took place the night you went missing, that would be great." He asked me if it was okay to talk with family in the room. I didn't mind.

I explained how someone kidnapped me from my garden and took me miles away into the woods. I explained how I fought for my life and killed the man who abducted me. Everyone's eyes were fixed on me as I told that horrible story. I saved the best part for last-the part when C-Lo told me how he killed Kayla and Matty. Tears were in my eyes when I told them how Kayla tried to protect her sister. "I got so angry because he had no remorse. It was like he was proud of what he had done. He tried to kill me! I had no choice but to fight back and kill him. He admitted to running over my friend, Mia. He said she shouldn't have been in the street."

"Was her name Mia Longwell?" Officer Stewart asked. I sat up more on my bed and took a deep breath. "Yes. Yes, it was. How did you know?"

"I was one of the first responders. We never found the person responsible." Wow, I couldn't believe it. How ironic was that? "So let me get this straight. The guy kidnapped you confessed to killing Matty, Kayla, Billy and his wife, and Mia Longwell?"

"Yes."

"This guy, what was his name?" asked Agent Doran.

"I never knew his real name, but he went by C-Lo." The two detectives looked at each other. Then Courtney said,

"You mean that wanna-be-pimp C-Lo?" OMG I just knew he was about to tell me that he knew him.

"Courtney, did you know him?" I asked.

"Yea, we grew up in the same neighborhood. He was always in trouble. When his dad killed his mom, he went crazy. His mom and my mom were the best of friends. I once sold him a car. He didn't want to pay me the rest of my money, so I went to his house. I told him I was gonna take him to court, then he finally gave it to me. He tried to give me one of his girls to have sex with." My jaw dropped, and I put my hand over my mouth. Then I said,

"Courtney, it was me he was taking about!"

"What, what are you talking about?"

"He had me locked in the room. I remember it like yesterday. Your exact words were 'you know that's not the kind of person I am.'"

"What the-you meant to tell me I could have saved you a long time ago!"

"Oh dear," said my grandma. Officer Stewart took out a photo of C-Lo and showed it to me.

"Is this him?" he asked. I took a good look. Indeed, it was him.

"Yes, that's him."

"His real name was Cory Lonez. He had previous arrests for assaulting woman and possession of illegal drugs. He also has a long record of DWI, and at one point, he was the prime suspect in Kayla and Matty's disappearance. We never could charge him because we had no hard evidence, and we never found the victims."

I told them exactly there to find them. Officer Doran got out his phone and stepped out. He came back in moments later and said he got a search team to go out and search the woods I was in. I noticed Courtney was looking out the window, as if he was sad about something. He was awfully quiet.

After about for hours, Detective Doran's phone ranged he informed his partner that they found the skeleton remains of two bodies. They still had to be sure, so they compared dental records. Eventually, they were able to do so. The skulls both had holes in them, confirming C-Lo's story that he shot them in the head. Officer Steward said to me, "You've solved a thirteen-year-old missing persons case."

Everyone in the room started clapping. The doctor came in and informed me that he wanted to keep me a few more days. He wanted to do more tests and observations. I'd been exposed to lots of things in the wood, so it only made sense.

So, for thirteen years, they had been trying to solve the mystery of what happened to Kayla and Matty. That was a long time. Now the family could get some closure. As the hours went by, nurses were coming in and out, checking vital signs drawing blood to check for rabies, etc. it was getting dark, and my parents were about to go home. They asked me if I wanted them to take Jan. I said no. I wanted my husband and my daughter to stay with me. When they left, Courtney and I had a long talk. "I'm sorry for hurting you, Courtney.", I said.

"I'm sorry for leaving you. I should have never left. This is all my fault." He held his head down in shame.

"No, baby. I messed up. I messed up pretty bad. I understand why you left. You were upset. I'm just glad he didn't kill you. He said he could have." It made sense to me now why C-Lo didn't kill him. He didn't kill Courtney because he knew him, lived in the same neighborhood and everything. Their mothers were friends. Small world. When Jan fell asleep, Courtney placed her on the visitor's bed by the window. He then got in the bed with me. I laid my head on is chest.

We continued to talk. We talked about how we were going to rebuild our marriage. We told each other we were gonna move on and let the past be the past. He had forgiven me for my infidelities. I vowed to not ever do something like that again. I love my husband and my daughter so much. I felt bad for Billy. I wish I could take back everything we did together. If I wanted to move on, I had to forgive myself and not dwell on it. In other words, I shouldn't live in the past.

The next day, Toa and Sandra came to visit me. I couldn't have been happier to see them. "Girl… I would have shot the bastard in his face!" said Sandra. Toa and I laughed. "How dare some asshole hurt our favorite chica!"

"I took care of business though," I said. "He wasn't gonna kill me. That was for sure.

"We're so proud of you," said Toa. "I gotta admit, I thought we lost you for a minute." They both came over and hugged me. Toa started crying. She made me and Sandra cry. They brought me get-well- balloons, cards, and flowers, and some of my favorite chocolate. I was healing pretty quickly. All the mosquito bites were gone, my lip and nose weren't no longer bloody, and my body wasn't dehydrated.

I was in the hospital for over a week before I was discharged. I recovered from my injuries and was ready to go. I took a nice shower, and Courtney brought my clothes. I was very excited to go back home and get back to my business and my life. I turned on the news in my hospital room. The news anchor was covering the story of how the Kayla and Matty's case was finally solved.

"You may remember the case of Kayla and Matty-the two sisters who went missing years ago." said the news anchor. "According to FBI agents and local law enforcement, the two girls' remains were found inside a shack located in the woods an hour and a half from the city. FBI agents said it was thanks to a local business woman who was abducted by the estranged killer and luckily got away. She shot and killed the perpetrator and struggled to find her way out of the woods. His name, was Cory Lonez." They showed a picture of him. "We were also informed that no charges will be filled against the woman as she is well protected under the Florida stand-your-your ground law."

Well, that was a relief. That story made breaking news. I was ready to go home and be with my family. "Are you ready baby?" Courtney asked.

"Yes, I'm ready." I finished putting my hair in curls, and we headed out. When we started the drive, I noticed we weren't headed in the direction of our house.

***

"Courtney, where are we going?" I asked.

"We have to make a quick stop first." To be honest, I just wanted to go home. I missed my couch, my bed, and most of all, my garden. I started to pitch a fit and tell him no and to just take me home. Instead, I just went with it. We pulled to this house that looked like a mini mansion. It was really big. The driveway was pretty huge. I figured this was his boss's house and he had a meeting or something. Connected to the house was a two-car garage. It looked like a little house itself. There were lots of cars parked on the street. Pretty soon, I was about to find out why. "Come on honey," he said.

"I'll wait until you're done with your meeting."

"It's gonna be a while, so you might wanna come in." I just said fine and went inside with him. When he opened the door, I was in front of family and friends, and they all yelled,

"SURPRISE!"

"Oh my God what is this!" I said, in total shock. Courtney grabbed my hand said,

Remember when I told you I had a surprise for you?"

"Yea," I said.

"Welcome, to our humble home." I was in a bit of a shock, trying to grasp what was going on.

"Are you trying to tell me this is our new house?" I asked.

"Exactly!"

I just held him and kissed him al over. Everyone was there-Toa, Sandra, my grandparents, my church family, Courtney's sister, and people from work. They had welcome-home banners up and balloons everywhere. Toa and Sandra ran up to me and said, "welcome home chica!" Then they hugged me. I hugged them back. My husband did this for me. He later told me he sold our old house and used the money to purchase this one. It was twice as big. We had a beautiful chandelier, a nice soft reddish carpet, marble floors in the kitchen and bathroom, and beautiful furniture.

Courtney grabbed my hand and said, "Come on, I wanna show you something." He took me out back, and my eyes got big. In front of me was a huge, beautiful garden. It was way bigger than my last garden. The patio area in the garden was also huge. You can almost fit a whole dinning set on it. Courtney threw a housewarming party that day. He invited lots of people. We barbecued and had lots of fun. "I have someone here who wants to meet you, honey," Courtney said. Then I was approached by a middle-aged couple holding two gifts. They introduced themselves as Mark and Annie Wolski-the parents of Kayla and Matty.

"We wanted to personally thank you for your bravery and your role in finding some closure for us," said Mark. Then he gave me the gift he had. I opened it up, and it was a brown-and-gold plaque with the beautiful picture of Kayla and Matty. Engraved on it, at the bottom, was the writing, THANK YOU AILINA MAYNORD! They then hugged me. Mrs. Wolski then gave her gift to me. I was a gold metal that said, THANK YOU FOR YOUR BRAVERY!

They were the sweetest couple ever. I had no idea I was gonna meet them. That was the best day of my life. God had been good to me even though I didn't deserve his grace and mercy. We all knew I should have been dead a long time ago. I'd come a long way. I went from a good girl turned bad, going to a mental institution and getting involved with a man who abused me and almost killed me. My prayers were heard and were answered the night I was kidnapped. I prayed hard that night in my garden. My husband forgave me, and I had my life back.

Two years later, I gave birth to another healthy baby girl. I named her after the oldest sister Kayla in honor of her bravery for protecting her sister. Sandra gave birth to a baby girl as well. Toa finally got married, and now she's pregnant. I am the godmother. We all decided to go on a vacation. We went to the Bahamas-me, Toa, Sandra, and our husbands and kids. I thank God I was able to have a second chance at life, and it took a simple prayer, a prayer in the garden.

A Prayer in the Garden